FAMILIAR OF THE WITCH

By Heather G. Harris

PUBLISHED BY HELLHOUND PRESS LIMITED

For my awesome supporters on Patreon, with special mention to Amanda Peterman and Melissa. I am so grateful and humbled by your belief in me.

Huge thanks as always, to my amazing ARC teams! I am so grateful for all you do to help me! Special mention to Jill Card Hazard for helping me refine Grimmy's language!

Content Warnings

Please see the full content warnings on Heather's website if you are concerned about triggers.

The *Portlock Paranormal Detective* series has poor language and scenes of violence.

Please note that all of Heather's works are written in British English with British phrases, spellings and grammar being utilised throughout. Jill has suffered through adding extra 'u's and shoving 's's everywhere instead of 'z's.

If you think you have found a typo, please do let Heather know here.

Foreword

If you'd like to hear the latest gossip, bargains and new releases from Heather, then please join Heather's VIP newsletter.

You can sign up here, and as a welcome gift you get some *free* books.

Chapter 1

'You're under arrest.'

I stared at Tristan's bodyguard, Mack. Magic-cancelling cuffs dangled in his hands. Glaring at him, I demanded, 'Is that really necessary? We both know that I'm going to be cleared of any wrongdoing in relation to Hilary's death.'

'That is not a foregone conclusion,' he disagreed gruffly. 'However, I am willing to cuff your hands in front of you.' He drawled it out like he was doing me a favour.

'How very kind of you,' I bit out snottily. 'Has anyone ever told you that you're the Monday of the human world?'

Mack's lips drew back in a snarl. Bastion's face was no less thunderous, but his rage was directed at the wizard trying to cuff me and he stepped towards Mack with violent intent. I sighed and held up a hand. 'Don't bother killing him,' I said. 'I need to deal with this head on. I'd rather not have the cuffs on, but we always knew I was going to be tried. The black witches are pulling the strings here.'

Bastion let me push him back but the threat of violence simmered in his now-golden eyes. He was *not* happy.

Mack's jaw tightened. 'This has nothing to do with black witches,' he spat. 'This has to do with you. You killed a member of the Coven Council. It cannot be borne.'

'She was a practising black witch,' I pointed out with exasperation.

'So *you* say.'

'So *she* said,' I countered. 'She confessed and I have a video of her confession.'

'Then you won't have any issue in the trial, will you?' he sneered.

That was what I hoped, but I'd long since learned not to count my ingredients until they were in the cauldron.

Mack stepped closer, holding out the cuffs. Bastion let out a low warning growl. 'I'll do it,' he snarled at Mack. 'You're not touching her.'

Mack blinked, but he didn't dare argue with the hulking griffin who was seething with rage and exuding barely leashed fury. I was pissed off as well, but apparently I wasn't anywhere near as intimidating. I needed to work on that.

I had been hoping to finish the final-defence potion for Bastion and Shirdal today; instead, it would have to remain under stasis until I came back. 'Wait one moment,' I said. My tone made it clear I wasn't asking. 'I'll just put this in stasis so the potion isn't ruined.'

Though I wasn't asking for his permission, Mack nodded as if I were. 'Fine.'

I leisurely painted *isa* on the cauldrons to keep the potion base stable. I'd have one week before the rune work broke down, and hopefully my trial would be over by then. And if it wasn't, I'd have bigger problems than just the final-defence potions.

I looked around and wished that Mack hadn't seen my private lab; it is exactly that, *private.* But I'd gotten sloppy; I was so used to Bastion and I wandering in and out that I hadn't secured the hidden entrance from my home office and Mack had just strolled in. It was an error I wouldn't be repeating. Assuming, of course, that I was subsequently freed and able to make mistakes again.

I wished I'd taken the time to visit Mum this morning, but I'd planned to go in the evening. Who knew how long it would be before I was back in the Home Counties and could see her?

Oscar and I try to visit Mum daily. Oscar and Benji were with her now while I was safe in the Coven's tower doing some potion work. Unfortunately, Mum's dementia-like symptoms were worsening and she hadn't been lucid once during the last five days. We'd been praying for a few moments of clarity so I could get the code to the CD she'd left me – but I also just wanted to talk to her. I missed her something chronic. She is a force of nature when she is present, and I miss her with all my heart.

And the CD was important because apparently it held blackmail material on my elusive father, Shaun. He was purportedly a black witch and everything I needed to find him was on an encrypted CD. All of that essential information was stuck behind a cursed passcode.

I'd tried everything I could think of to unlock it: my name, my date of birth, Mum's familiar Lucille's date of birth, Oscar's details ... all that and more. Nothing had worked.

Of course Bastion knew a hacker, but he wasn't currently available. Bastion said that meant he was off somewhere doing some sort of black ops. We either needed the hacker to return or for Mum to have a lucid day, but so far neither had happened – now I was being arrested.

Impatience roared through me. I had so much to do and none of it involved dealing with this nonsense about Hilary's death. People were depending on me. 'I'll just send a couple of emails,' I said abruptly to Mack. Again, I wasn't asking for his permission.

His mouth tightened but he didn't stop me when I opened my laptop. I sent a quick email to Jeb, Ethan and Jacob, outlining the problem and asking them to take over running the Coven for me *again*. Then I sent a brief Coven-wide email explaining about my arrest as briefly and unemotionally as possible. I said it was just a formality and I'd be back soon. I hoped I wasn't lying.

'Okay,' I said to Bastion as I shut the laptop. 'You can cuff me.' I held out my hands. He was right: I'd rather he did it than Mack.

Anger radiated from every inch of Bastion's body; I needed to distract my ferocious bodyguard or one wrong word from Mack would see his guts decorating my walls. And Jeb had only repainted them a couple of weeks ago.

Bastion gently secured the cuffs around my wrist, leaving plenty of room so they didn't bite into my skin. I swayed as the cuffs closed and my magic was ripped away from me. The feeling of emptiness was so sudden, so stark, that I struggled for a moment to hide my panic. Even when I was in the Common, the non-magical realm, I still had a tendril of magic but now I had none. The potion bomb in my pocket would be completely useless to me. I felt raw, naked and defenceless and I totally despised that feeling.

I raised my chin defiantly. I was without my magic but I wasn't weak.

Bastion was watching me, his eagle eyes missing nothing. His jaw tightened at my poorly hidden distress. 'I'm okay,' I lied softly for his ears alone. 'Though I have to say this isn't quite how I'd envisioned you cuffing me.' I waggled my eyebrows suggestively and willed him to let me lighten the mood.

I saw the moment that he decided to let me have my way. A small smile tugged at his lips. 'Fluffy ones,' he breathed into the shell of my ear.

My cheeks heated. We still hadn't even exchanged so much as a kiss because the moment had never felt right. Now I wholeheartedly regretted that omission. Well, at least while I was in prison I'd have the image of Bastion twirling black fluffy cuffs to keep my blood hot.

And if the other inmates bothered me? They'd soon learn that I was nobody's bitch.

Chapter 2

Mack refused to let Bastion fly in the helicopter with me; the wizard clearly had a death wish. Bastion's eyes were golden and his shift was close to the surface. I shook my head briskly, silently ordering him *not* to kill the foolish man. I might not have liked Mack's actions but he was just doing his job. Albeit badly and rudely.

As Mack strapped me in, Bastion stood nearby watching to make sure no excessive force was used. Once upon a time, he'd been hired by the Council to protect me, though these days I suspected that Oscar was his paymaster. That was a relief because it meant that Bastion was following my orders rather than the Council's.

I was relieved that Oscar wasn't here to see me arrested. Bastion had managed to keep a level head – at my behest – but Oscar had all-but raised me after my own father had abandoned me. He wouldn't have let Mack take me, and who knew how a fight between the two of them would have gone?

Oscar was in his sixties now; though he showed no signs of slowing down, I had recurring nightmares about him getting hurt on the job. Not long ago he'd been knocked out and concussed and that had brought home the fact that he wasn't a spring chicken any more. Even so, I knew that making him retire would hurt him as much as the blow to the head had done.

Mack closed the helicopter door with an ominous thunk. If he thought that making Bastion stay behind would inconvenience the griffin or prove an obstacle to him, he was even thicker than he looked. There was no way Bastion would let Mack take me to some black-ops site without following every inch of the way. I knew my griffin; there was no chance he'd let me be taken anywhere but Edinburgh for the trial that Mack had spoken about.

Instead of brutally murdering Mack, Bastion shifted into his griffin form. As the helicopter took off, so did he. I grinned as I saw his huge white wings soaring next to us.

'Lose him,' Mack grunted to the pilot.

In fairness to the pilot he did try, but no matter how much he ducked and dived he couldn't shake Bastion. The ride was bumpy as hell as the helicopter twisted and turned but, despite the aerial acrobatics, my griffin stuck to us like glue. I smirked at Mack, no doubt making his blood pressure rise.

After fifteen minutes of aerial tag, Mack gave a barely audible sigh. 'He's not going anywhere. Just get us to Edinburgh as fast as possible.' I wondered if that was a change in destination or not.

I managed not to snicker aloud, but I struggled not to grin. The rest of the journey was significantly smoother and I entertained myself by watching Bastion through the window. Even in griffin form he was a magnificent specimen. His corded muscles bunched and rolled as he flew easily next to the helicopter, keeping pace with us without a hint of effort.

I tried my best to stay loose and relaxed; one sign of tension from me and Bastion would probably tear open the helicopter doors and rescue me. Though I enjoyed the image, I was nobody's damsel in distress – not even his.

Before long, we were landing on top of The Witchery restaurant and hotel, which is the witches' headquarters. We take hiding in plain sight seriously.

Mack opened the door, unstrapped me, took my arm and dragged me from the helicopter. Bastion let out an eagle shriek of pure rage and landed with a resounding whump that rocked through the building. I smiled. I'd ridden on Bastion's back and I knew his landings were usually feather light. He was being heavy-footed on purpose. He was so sweet.

Mack swallowed hard but continued to drag me inside as Bastion shimmered into human form. Not for the first time, I thought it was a shame that he managed to retain his clothes when he shifted. His eyes, now blazing like suns, followed my every movement. He stalked down the stairs behind me; his presence at my back as reassuring as ever.

Rosemary, the maître d' of The Witchery, glared at Mack then gave me a little bow and touched her hand to her heart as I was marched down into the bowels of the building. That small sign of solidarity strengthened me. I was not without allies.

I was taken down into the underground city. At the gate stood ten wizards, all with weapons drawn. 'You go no further,' Mack ordered Bastion, unable to hide his triumph.

A laugh slipped out before I could stop it. Bastion can *coax*. If you have the slightest inclination to do something, Bastion can fan that whim into action. If one of the guards hated another, he could get them to kill each other. If the wizards were secretly trembling in the face of the deadliest assassin to walk the earth, he could make them run away. Or he could simply slice them to pieces with his beak and his talons. No matter what they believed, the wizards guarding the entrance were no barrier to Bastion.

That thought made me frown; killing them all wouldn't exactly start my trial off on the right foot. I met Bastion's dark eyes and reluctantly shook my head. 'Stay,' I entreated him, not an order but a request.

Mack laughed. 'Sit. Stay. There's a good boy,' he mocked. I grimaced, the man was not only a fool, he had no sense of self-preservation. I had half a mind to let Bastion tear into him just to teach him a lesson.

Bastion levelled a look at Mack that a more sensible man would have recognised as a death threat. Mack sneered. I had tried to save his life, but implying to an Other creature that they were a pet...?

Human–creature relations are touch and go at the best of times, but lately they'd been rockier than usual since some more vocal members of the Symposium had tried to pass a law tagging all Other creatures as if they were cattle.

Bastion was furious, and I didn't blame him. Mack had passed from 'just doing his job' territory and danced right into 'Schadenfreude asshole' land. Bastion was going to slice and dice him like a teriyaki chef.

My arrest was an unfortunate misunderstanding. Yes, I'd killed Hilary – but she had killed Abigay. Under Coven rules, I was well within my rights to avenge the Crone. This mess would be cleared up in no time. Hopefully. But Mack? His fate was sealed. In the Other realm, each species has their own rules and regulations and one of those is that griffins don't ignore insults. Goodbye, Mack – I won't miss you.

He grabbed my arm tightly and I bit back the cry that tried to escape at his sudden use of force. Bastion stepped forward, lips twisted in a snarl. I shook my head again firmly then smiled, hoping that would be enough to stop him killing anyone. 'Don't,' I said to him. 'Not yet,' I amended. That made Bastion smile darkly and look at my captor with anticipation. Bastion enjoys anticipation.

He met my eyes and inclined his head slightly. *Not yet,* he silently agreed.

Mack hauled me away from Bastion into the dark depths of the dead city. I held my griffin's gaze for as long as I could, hating the thought of being without him. He'd been my shadow for weeks and with him near me I felt safe, even when the whole world seemed to be gunning for me. Without him, I hated how bereft I felt. I'm not weak and I don't *need* anybody – but I definitely *wanted* him.

Mack left the other wizards behind, no doubt to hold back Bastion. Fools: they'd have been better trying to stop the tide. I had no doubt he'd find another way into the underground city because the only order he would obey was not to massacre the guards.

I'd expected to be taken straight to the Coven Council but instead I was escorted to a dank cell, one in a row of five. None of the others were occupied. There was no natural light and the two torches of burning oil offered meagre light. Cosy.

There was nothing in the corridor bar the cells, and there were no other guards in sight. The wizards were relying on magic-cancelling cuffs and steel bars to confine me. That was lazy.

I sniffed. 'You have got to be kidding me,' I said to Mack, wishing my hands were free so that I could put them on my hips to reinforce my disapproval. 'This hovel is *not* appropriate accommodation.'

'Don't make me push you in, *hula witch,*' he snarled. The gleam in his eyes suggested that he wanted an excuse to do just that, so I pressed my lips together in a firm line and swanned in like it was the Ritz. I blithely ignored his pathetic insult. I was proud of my use of hula hoops in salt circles and frankly, the insult made me smile every time.

I turned to face him as he clanged the cell door shut behind me. The door was made of metal bars, giving me no privacy whatsoever. 'Mack,' I called as he started to walk away.

He turned back to face me. 'What?'

I smiled. 'I won't forget this.' And, more importantly, neither would Bastion.

'I don't give a fuck what you remember. Hilary was a friend of mine.'

Mack was a wizard but that didn't mean he wasn't working for the black Coven. 'Are you employed by black witches, Mack? No one else is around. You can tell me the truth.'

'Fuck you,' he spat. 'Hilary was the kindest witch I've ever met. I won't have you tarnish her good name. She was innocent and you're a murderess. You're going to live in these dungeons for the rest of your life, so get used to it.' He stalked out.

His outrage seemed real; he really did believe in Hilary's innocence. How cute. So he wasn't working for the black Coven, then; he was just your average ignorant asshole. I rarely swear – even within the confines of my own head – but that man deserved that moniker.

I looked around. The underground city, known as 'the dead city' by the witches, is cold and dark. We have electricity and running water down here nowadays but it looked like my damp dwelling had neither. Wonderful.

Mack hadn't bothered to search me. Perhaps his rage had made him incompetent, or maybe he was just bad at his job. Perhaps he believed that, cuffed as I was, I could do no damage. He was wrong.

My athame was strapped to my ankle, hidden by my swishing, full-length skirt. It is highly unusual for a witch to arm herself; after all, that's why we hire wizards as bodyguards. With the wizards' skill in the IR – the intention and release – they have powerful magic at their fingertips that we simply can't compete with. We only have runes and potions that are time-consuming to produce and activate.

But someone had been trying to kill me for weeks and only a fool remains unarmed in those circumstances. My blade reassured me a little. With my magic ripped away I felt vulnerable, but I wasn't wholly without my defences. I had cold hard steel – and a potion bomb in my skirt pocket. Without my magic to activate it, it was as much use as a fire elemental at sea but I still I felt better knowing it was there.

I paced around the small cell that was only three metres by three metres. My mattress was thin, hard and narrower than a single bed. My toilet was a bucket. There was no sink. The place was absolutely disgusting. The Council would be hearing about this.

I strode around the cell – I refused to call it a room – fifty times. When I'd dissipated some of my nervous energy, I sat on the bed. It wasn't long until the cold penetrated my limbs and I started to shiver.

Bastion had been removed from my side. With the black witches desperate for my blood, now was the perfect opportunity for them to strike. I wished I'd had more sleep last night. Goddess knew, I wouldn't be getting any tonight.

Chapter 3

I was jerked awake as someone whispered my name. Damn it, I wasn't supposed to be sleeping. I opened my gritty eyes and peered into the darkness. The electric-blue backpack was obvious even in the dark.

'Kass?' I whispered in surprise, 'What are you doing here?'

'Amber, I am so sorry.' She was wringing her hands. 'This is a farce.'

'That's exactly how I feel about it,' I muttered grumpily.

'Are you okay?'

'I've been better.' I yawned. 'What time is it?'

'It's 3am. I'm sorry to wake you but I snuck in when Mack swapped shifts. Daryl let me in. He thinks you're innocent.'

'Daryl...' My mind was blank for a moment then my sleepy neurons started to fire, 'Willow's guard?'

'Yes.'

I grimaced. 'If he's guarding me, who is guarding Willow? Get some of the enforcers on the guard rotation. We can't afford to have the Council members vulnerable to attack.'

Kass shook her head in disbelief. 'I can't believe you're worrying about them when they've arrested you. This is all Seren's doing. We all know you're innocent but she's convinced everyone that a trial will clear you, that it's in your best interests.'

She bit her nail then went on. 'It took me ages to find you here – in the dungeons, of all places! It's an outrage! I tried to get you moved but, given the late hour when you arrived, that was nixed. Listen, I overheard Seren talking to someone and she said she had more charges to level at you. I don't know what they are. Any ideas?'

I smiled ruefully. I run a secret clinic and give away healing for free, I'm involved with a circus that helps people escape the yoke of the Connection, and I possess a sentient grimoire. All three are highly illegal and I wondered which one Seren had discovered. My money was on the clinic because I'd recently turned up there with Bastion on my heels and he was pretty well known. With hindsight that hadn't been my wisest move, but I'd gone to the clinic on the back of a really long day. Even I make mistakes now and again, but if Seren had her way that particular one might cost me everything.

I kept my self-recrimination off my face. 'Some,' I said simply. 'How is Bastion?'

Kass winced. 'He's furious the Council won't let him visit you.' She paused. 'Don't take this the wrong way. I know you like him, but he's a little scary.'

Calling Bastion a little scary was like calling a hurricane a light breeze. I shrugged. 'He grows on you.'

Kass opened her backpack. 'Here.' She passed me a flask through the bars. 'Hot chocolate.' Next she pulled a Tupperware box out. 'Some overnight oats. It's not much, but it was all I could scrounge that wouldn't be disgusting cold.'

My tummy gave a loud rumble as I gratefully took the box. 'Thank you.' I felt a lump in my throat; I'd never had someone come through for me like this before. There again, I'd never been arrested before either. 'I appreciate it.'

Kass rubbed her wrists as if they were sore. Her fibromyalgia often flared up at times of stress making her joints ache. Having me arrested and thrown in jail was probably a bit stressful for her, too. I grimaced. That was another thing to lay at Mack and Seren's doors.

I ate as quickly as I could with my hands bound in front of me in the damned cuffs. The smell of food had made me realise I was incredibly hungry. I painstakingly took the lid off the hot chocolate thermos – tricky in cuffs – but when Kass tried to help me, I shot her a glare. I needed to do this for myself.

She waited until the lid was off then held out a mug for me to pour it into. It was a white mug and even in the poor light I could make out the words scrawled across it: *This too shall pass.* I took a deep breath. Damn right. Everything is transient: the good, the bad and the ugly. This was the latter, but it would pass.

I poured the hot chocolate into the mug, then gave her the flask and lid so I could seize the mug instead. I wrapped my fingers around it, luxuriating in the warmth that spread through my fingers, and took a tentative sip. It was the perfect temperature. It warmed me up in more ways than one. 'Nice hot chocolate,' I complimented her.

'Bastion made it for you. He melted in some chocolate flakes.'

The rock in my throat was back. Bastion had sent me hot chocolate. No doubt he was the one behind the mug too. Not too long ago, I'd been a tea girl but when I'd been poisoned through a cup of tea, my drink of choice had been shelved. One day it would be dusted off again but not yet. In the meantime, I'd adopted hot chocolate.

'Pass him my thanks, won't you?' I tried to keep my voice level but it wobbled a little.

Kass tried to lighten the mood. 'Do you want me to pass him anything else?' She twitched her eyebrows, trying to get me to laugh.

I managed a smile. 'No thanks.'

Why hadn't I kissed Bastion in the last five days? I should have done it when we were being guarded in Rosie's while I re-charged. With other guards around, that had probably been the closest to relaxed that I'd seen him. I should have kissed him then, but I'd chickened out.

Instead, here I was in a jail cell pondering my few regrets. Not kissing Bastion was one of them – the main one, really. I supposed it was a good thing that, at this stage of my life, I'd come to realise that regrets weren't all that much help. Do, or do not. Don't regret. Except kissing Bastion, I regretted not doing that. There was something between us that deserved exploration.

I contemplated giving Kass a message for Bastion, but none of my half-formed thoughts did justice to the maelstrom in my heart. I struggle at the best of times to vocalise my feelings, and this wasn't the best of times.

'Just tell him to make sure he has back-up video footage of Hilary's confession ready.' I had no doubt the original footage would 'accidentally' go walkabout if Mack had his way.

'Already on it,' she promised.

I passed Kass the empty Tupperware and flask. Regretfully, I also passed back the empowering mug. 'We'd better not leave any evidence of your visit. Thanks for coming, Kass. I really do appreciate it.'

'What are friends in high places for if not for visiting you when you're in dire straits?'

I cut off the 'getting you out of trouble in the first place?' comment that wanted to slip out. Kass was new to the Council and it was run democratically. Mack was Tristan's guard so Tristan was clearly against me, and Seren had hated me since we were kids. I hoped the others were being washed along with some 'good intentions'. I'd have to remind them all that while good *intentions* pave the path to hell, it is good *actions* that count. Hopefully the trial would put an end to the whole sordid mess.

I studied my tired friend. 'How are you, Kass?'

She looked at me, startled. '*I'm* okay. I'm not the one in a jail cell.'

'You were rubbing your wrists. Flare up?'

She sighed. 'Yeah, a little.' She was downplaying it; she was holding herself stiffly and I could tell she was in pain.

'Have you tried taking 4312?' Some potions have names but all of them have a numeric designation. I wished to heck I'd stuck with numbers rather than naming my ORAL potion. Live and learn.

Kass frowned. 'Isn't 4312 a muscle-building potion? For use after long-term comas?'

'Yes, but I've been researching fibromyalgia and exercise comes up frequently as something that helps. It makes sense that 4312 might have some positive effects.'

She blinked. 'I've never thought of that. I'll definitely try it.' She gave me a rueful smile. 'I'll try anything at this point. Pain management only does so much.'

'Yeah, that sucks.' Although I am bad at verbalising my feelings, she deserved my best efforts so I tried. 'You do so much for so many. Your Coven admire you – *I* admire you. Some people in your circumstances would fall down and they wouldn't get back up. But you ... you keep on going. I admire that a great deal.'

Kass looked away. When she looked back at me, there were tears in her eyes. 'Thank you. I appreciate that more than you know.' She cleared her throat. 'I feel like a fraud having the membership seat,' she confessed in a wobbly voice. 'It should have been you.'

'We all battle imposter syndrome now and again, even me. You deserve the seat,' I said firmly. 'You earned it. I trust you to use it for the betterment of witches everywhere. Now, you'd better go. I don't want you getting caught. Mack will be back soon, no doubt. Tell Bastion I'm okay, alright?'

'I will. Hang in there, Amber. The trial starts in the morning. Get some more sleep.'

With the food and drink warming me, I planned to do nothing of the sort. After all, the witching hours were for plotting. I touched the kiss mark that the imp Frogmatch had once given me. It was time to call in some favours.

Chapter 4

I watched Frogmatch disappear through the bars and move off, his little claws clacking on the cold flagstones. Dawn was still an hour or two away as I huddled on the pathetic excuse for a bed, hoping my plans with the imp would bear fruit.

I was still sitting there, shivering, when a vampyr phased into my cell. A scream slipped out of my throat before I could quash it. My bound hands fumbled with my skirts, wrenching them out of the way to grasp the hilt of my athame.

The vampyr hovered before me, waiting almost patiently for me to produce my weapon. His eyes were leached to black; he was being controlled by a necromancer.

I raised my athame. With my wrists bound, I had no option but to adopt a two-handed grip. My heart was thundering, but I struggled not to show my fear as I shot to my feet so I had room to manoeuvre. But even with the best will in the world, I knew I couldn't beat a vampyr, not with their lightning reflexes and super speed. Not when I could barely hold a weapon. I wished for magic with all of my heart, but nothing came.

The vampyr smiled and its teeth were blood red. 'Hello, my daughter. You've been looking for me.' His voice was a low groan, discordant, like the words were being pushed unwillingly out of a bagpipe.

A chill ran down my spine. My father was controlling the vampyr! Goddess, my mum's fears hadn't been unfounded. My father wasn't just a black witch; he was a necromancer.

'You're a necromancer,' I stated the obvious aloud.

'Yes,' he said a moment later using the vampyr's rattling, wheezing breath. 'You could be great too, Amber. You've done well and I'm very proud of you, but you could be even greater than you are. You have so much potential that it glitters in you, my child, but you have only scratched the surface of your worth.'

'I know what I'm worth,' I disagreed. 'Nothing will make me kill for power.'

A huffing broken sound bubbled from the vampyr's lips and it took me a moment to realise that he was laughing. Revulsion swept through me.

'You'd be surprised what you will do, Amber. Perhaps not for power but for love. I see the way you look at Bastion. What would you do to keep him safe?'

Anything. An icy shiver slid down my spine and fear pricked my scalp. My father – whoever he was – had been watching me closely enough to know that I had feelings for Bastion. It wasn't love. It was just ... loneliness, the need for companionship. Bastion was yin to my yang but that didn't mean anything. It didn't mean love.

'Bastion doesn't need me to keep him safe,' I retorted.

'That may be right, daughter, that may be right. But perhaps one day there will be the pitter-patter of tiny feet and then we'll see what you wouldn't do for your children.'

I didn't tell him that I didn't want children; he didn't deserve to have that knowledge about me. 'Don't pretend that you became a necromancer for me. You *left* me.'

'I was forced to!' The words came out in a furious snarl and a drop of the vampyr's bloody red spit landed on my cheek. I forced myself not to wipe it away and to hold the blade steady.

'You could have sworn to have stayed a white witch instead of twisting further into darkness,' I argued. Then I changed tack. 'Was it you who attacked my mother?'

The vampyr's head twitched sharply. 'None of the attacks on your mother were designed to harm her.'

For some reason I believed him. 'Then what *were* they designed to do?' I asked impatiently.

The vampyr smiled. 'I've no doubt you'll find out soon enough. You're fairly implacable once you get started.' His head twitched violently to the other side and blue eyes flashed at me for a moment, full of horror and revulsion.

'Tsch,' my father uttered from his borrowed voice box. 'This one is a fighter. Too bad. Never mind. I'll get another.' The vampyr's eyes fixed on my athame. 'I'm glad to see you're keeping the athame safe, Amber. Keep it on you at all times. It is not a trinket.'

My jaw clenched. The athame was a family heirloom, but until now I hadn't thought to ask which side of the family it had come from. Was it from my mother's side? Or my father's?

My father interrupted my thoughts. 'Look lively, Amber, here he comes! A crucible of fire, and you'll come out stronger than ever.' Then the vampyr's eyes were black again and he leapt towards me, moving with supernatural speed. His fangs snapped out.

Death was only moments away and I froze with fear, holding my athame out awkwardly in my manacled hands.

With a gurgling laugh, the black-eyed vampyr jumped on to the athame and pierced his own heart. He hung there for a moment, stuck on my blade as I stared in horror. Then the vampyr's eyes faded to blue, he smiled a little and stilled.

'I'm sorry,' I managed to say as he disappeared in a puff of dust and ash.

I tried to tell myself that my father had killed him, not me, but the athame in my hands was coated in thick red blood. It dripped towards my hands, staining them like the stain that was growing on my soul.

Chapter 5

I heard footsteps before I saw Mack. Luckily, I was prepared. I had already swept the dusty remains of the vampyr into the toilet bucket with my bare hands. He had exploded into ash right in front of me and, though I'd done my best to brush him off, I had ash marks across my clothes, hands and face. The struggle had also torn my skirt and my blouse and I'd also ripped the skirt in my haste to free the athame.

I had no doubt that I looked even more neglected than I felt. My discomposure wasn't far from the truth, but now it was visible to the world. So often in life we keep our wounds invisible, but that wouldn't do me any good today. I needed the masses on my side, so I would let some vulnerability show. Not that I had a whole lot of choice.

Mack either didn't care about my unkempt appearance or he didn't notice. My money was on the former; he was ex-army and he was an observant man. 'Move,' he grunted as he clanged the cell door open. His eyes swept over me and his jaw tightened but he said nothing. If he could tell I'd battled and killed a vampyr, would that make him think I was more evil or less?

I stood. 'Can I get some food and water?' Thanks to Kass's visit, I didn't particularly need either, though a bit of H2O is always welcome. Hydration is important. What I wanted was a refusal from him that I could use later.

'No. Move,' he growled.

Bingo. 'Charming,' I muttered as I made my way out of the cell. Once again he grabbed my upper arm, yanking me forcefully. I winced as he pressed against the bruises he'd made yesterday. 'You're such a gentleman,' I said sarcastically.

Perhaps riling your jailor wasn't wise, but no one has ever accused me of being wise.

'You're no lady,' he bit back.

He continued to drag me forwards. I was surprised when he pulled me not towards the Council's chambers, as I'd expected, but to the witches' hall. A new golem was standing on the door. He was as hulking as Benji, but he didn't smile as he caught sight of me.

'Hello,' I greeted him curiously. 'I'm Amber DeLea. What's your name?'

'David Abrams,' he responded shortly.

'Are you newly awakened?' I pried, though I already knew the answer.

'Yes – since you stole the last golem.' His tone was accusing. Yeesh, he'd been awake a few days and he'd already decided I was persona non grata.

'I didn't steal him. Benji is my friend.'

David's eyebrows rose. 'You're friends – with a golem?' His tone was incredulous.

'Yes, why shouldn't I be?'

Surprise danced across his features as he looked at me afresh. He parted his lips to speak but Mack got there first. 'Abrams,' he interrupted us with a scowl. 'Announce us.' He glared. 'Now.'

David's eyes flashed red then back to brown. 'All clear,' he confirmed. As he pushed open the door behind him, he slid me a sideways glance and I smiled encouragingly. He cleared his throat. 'Announcing the arrival of the witch, Coven Mother, Rune Mistress and Potion Mistress Amber DeLea.'

His voice boomed into the hall and it fell gratifyingly silent. Maybe David *had* warmed to me just a little, because it was unusual to announce a prisoner's full titles like that. My smile widened and he gave me a small nod in return.

I looked into the hall and let my jaw drop as if I were surprised. Truthfully, I was a little. Despite my machinations, I hadn't been sure my allies would be able to pull off my plan but it looked like they had.

The hall was crammed to the rafters. It normally had a capacity of two to three hundred, but it was so packed that there seemed to be even more. I had no idea how Frogmatch had done it, but he'd brought in witches from all over the country. No matter what I'd done for the imp, the scales had swung back in his favour. I owed him.

The Council were sitting on a raised dais. I was pleased to see that they all had their cowls down – and that they all looked a little unnerved by the number of witches crammed into the room.

Mack continued to drag me forward. I let my body droop and my feet slow a little, making him drag me all the more viciously.

I caught sight of Jeb, Ethan and Jacob across the hall. What on earth were they doing here? That wasn't part of the plan! Who was running my damned Coven in their absence? Then I saw more of my Coven: Melrose, Venice,

John. Half of them were here. Had Frogmatch cajoled them in the early hours of the morning, or had they come in response to my Coven-wide email. Were they here to support me or to condemn me? I hoped the former, but my self-doubt whispered the latter.

Angry mutterings sprang up as the crowd took in my tousled hair and clothing and the way in which Mack was manhandling me. 'What is the meaning of this?' Willow asked loudly. 'Why does Amber look like a prisoner? Why on earth is she wearing magic-cancelling cuffs?'

Tristan frowned. 'She killed Hilary. She is dangerous.' Crikey, nothing like being innocent until being proven guilty, hey?

'She killed a *black* witch!' Willow countered.

'So *she* says!' Tristan batted back.

'We have already heard from quite a few other witnesses this morning who also say so!' Willow responded sharply.

'DeLea's driver and bodyguard is bound to support her,' Tristan bickered. 'He didn't see the killing blow, and Rosemary didn't see anything directly either. Nor did Benjamin Cohen, since he had been powered down by *her* hand.' He stabbed his finger at me.

'Even so, all three were on the chair of truth and all three swore that Hilary confessed to being a black witch. Unless you're suggesting that they could somehow circumvent my runes?' Willow glared as she challenged him.

Tristan backed down a little; even he wasn't foolish enough to suggest her runes weren't effective. 'I'm saying those witnesses could be mistaken but still *believe* they were speaking the truth.'

I was suddenly quite pleased not to be a part of the Council. Frankly, this sniping in front of everyone was embarrassing.

Jasper clearly agreed. 'Enough!' he called. 'Bring Miss DeLea to the chair and let the questioning commence.'

Mack continued to haul me forward before depositing me on a chair that was placed on a pentagram. The pentagram was unconcealed and filled with truth-compulsion runes. Lovely: I was about to spill my guts about anything they asked me. I hoped they wouldn't ask too many questions and that I didn't incriminate myself with my answers. I had to think carefully about my responses; I would need to keep a level head under the choking weight of the truth runes.

Easy.

'I'll go first,' Bastion said loudly as he strode onto the hall's floor. He lifted me effortlessly out of the chair and sat down on it instead.

'What are you doing?' I asked out of the side of my mouth.

'Saving you,' he murmured. He inhaled my scent. 'You smell of vampyr, Bambi. Are you okay? I felt your fear.' His voice was clipped and taut with anger; he hated that he hadn't been there to save me during the night, though he was keen to remedy that now.

I hadn't needed him to save me last night because my father was controlling the vampyr like a puppet on a string and he had stuffed his marionette onto my blade. I couldn't have avoided killing him if I'd tried. My father had wanted the pugnacious vampyr to die and he'd used me to do it.

'I'm okay,' I reassured Bastion. 'What's your plan?'

He didn't answer directly. 'You have too many secrets to be questioned on this chair. Keep your game face on.'

I had no game face, but I did my best to summon – and maintain – my haughtiest expression.

Tristan was glowering at Bastion. 'You have not yet been summoned to give evidence. You—'

'Give it a rest, Tristan,' Beatrice snapped. 'Let the griffin say his piece and then we can hear from DeLea, if necessary.' When Beatrice had been attacked and injured by a black witch masquerading as Felix, I had healed her injuries. It seemed she was warmly disposed towards me, which was a nice surprise because she'd always struck me as wholly glacial before this.

Tristan subsided and sat back sulkily in his chair. Bastion calmly and dispassionately related the events that had led to Hilary's death: the fake text that said Abigay had confiscated dark artefacts in her rooms and Hilary subsequently tearing the place apart to look for them. Then Bastion explained that Hilary had confessed to being a necromancer and that she had summoned and controlled three vampyrs in front of him.

The hall was completely silent as the witches hung on his every word so silently you could have heard a rune stone drop. I held on to my haughty expression and waited for the punchline. To be honest, I had no idea where he was going with this because with the next few sentences he would say that I had killed Hilary. Regardless of his best efforts, once he uttered those words I would be questioned on that chair.

Bastion looked Tristan squarely in the eyes. 'Hilary came to attack me. She drew a poisoned athame and she stabbed me with it. I killed her.'

I blinked. No way! There was *no way* he should have been able to say that whilst sitting on so many truth runes.

He hadn't killed her, *I* had. It took a huge amount of effort for me to remain impassive.

Tristan faltered. 'You killed her?'

'I killed her,' Bastion lied firmly. 'I sliced open her throat.'

What. The. Heck.

Chapter 6

'I have footage,' Bastion continued.

'Regretfully,' Tristan started with a sneer, 'the footage Miss DeLea supplied was corrupted.'

Bastion smiled, though there was nothing friendly about it. 'Luckily I had several copies made. Just in case of any regrettable incompetence.' The insult was laid out there, spat at Tristan. The witch flushed but said nothing.

That was Benji's cue. He rolled in a huge TV and placed it on the dais so that everyone crowding into the hall could see it. He gave me a grin and a thumbs-up, which I couldn't help returning, then he turned on the TV and pressed a few buttons. The footage started rolling.

'And besides,' I said pointedly, 'it's the Crone position that you covet, isn't it?'

Hilary's eyes narrowed. 'I don't especially like your tone. What are you implying, Amber?'

'I'm not implying anything. I'm saying you want to be the next Crone, don't you?'

'What gave me away?' Hilary asked calmly, as her eyes leached to black.

The whole room was engrossed as our conversation reached boiling point.

'Benji is worth his weight in gold,' I said.

'Oh, he is,' she agreed. 'To the right person. Luckily, that person is me. His obedience to the Council is absolute.' She fixed her eyes on Benji, expression triumphant. 'Benji, kill Bastion.'

The footage stopped and I tried to keep the frown off my face. It had been expertly spliced to ensure there was no mention of the black Coven at any point – no need to start mass hysteria – but it ended before it showed who *had* killed Hilary.

Bastion spoke into the shocked silence. 'As you can see, she confessed to killing the Crone.'

Suddenly sound roared around the room as hundreds of voices started talking at once.

'She killed the Crone!'

'Hilary Mitchell! A black witch!'

'She was always a bitch.'

'Silence!' Tristan roared. The witches paid him no attention; they were too busy being shocked and gossiping at what had been revealed. I heard the word 'necromancer'; No one had missed the way Hilary's eyes had leached to black.

Frogmatch had done a great job sourcing a huge TV that could be wheeled in because now everyone in the room had seen the footage and it was undeniable. This wasn't something Tristan could hush up; there were far too many witnesses. Tristan couldn't do anything but dismiss the charges against me.

I knew he wouldn't bring them against Bastion: firstly, he wouldn't dare, and secondly, the drums had beaten out over Calton Hill declaring war on the Crone's killer. Hilary had confessed and the sentence for killing a Crone was death. Bastion had said he had acted as judge, jury and executioner. There would be no reprisals.

It was with a decidedly sour look on his face that Tristan announced, 'The charges against Amber DeLea are dismissed.'

'Wait!' Seren cried. 'I have more charges to bring!'

Chapter 7

'This is highly irregular.' Beatrice glowered at Seren. 'All charges must be brought to the Council and discussed before they are ratified and levelled at the accused. You have not carried out due process.'

'We've all heard of Ellie Tron, the witch that heals without charging!' Seren cried, 'It's her! It's Amber!'

Kass stood. 'This whole thing has been nothing more than a witch hunt!' We rarely used that emotionally charged term, and there were audible gasps around the room.

My friend was new and she risked much by openly defying the other members of the Council so early in her career. She didn't care. She continued. 'A campaign is being waged to discredit an honourable witch. Amber DeLea has been weeding out black witches, so it seems to me that anyone levelling charges against her needs to be closely examined.

Whether intentionally or not, you are serving the black witches with this continued campaign of hatred and misinformation.'

'Me?' Seren squawked. 'I'm not a black witch! I'm telling you, *she's* Ellie Tron.' She pointed at me accusingly. I kept my face as blank as possible.

Kass and Bastion had tried, but the excrement was going to hit the fan. Once I was on that runed chair...

Melrose and Venice moved closer to me in a silent show of support that warmed my heart. Things had been rocky between Melrose and me ever since I had sequestered Meredith and Ria, but there was no hostility now.

I met her eyes. I don't know what she saw in mine but she nodded once, decisively, then turned to Venice. 'Have you ever seen the movie *Spartacus?*'

Venice's eyes went wide. 'Yes! Great idea.' She stood. 'I'm Spartacus!' she announced loudly to the hall.

'Fuck's sake,' Melrose muttered. She stood. 'I'm Ellie Tron!'

On the other side of the room, Jeb stood. 'I'm Ellie Tron!' he declared.

Isadora Moonspell stood, meeting my eyes as she cried, 'I'm Ellie Tron!'

John Melton stood. 'I'm Ellie Tron!' He grinned at me across the room.

And that was it. Suddenly twenty – thirty – fifty witches were on their feet declaring they were Ellie Tron. I struggled not to react. My game face was a thing of the past as the whole room roared the name of my alter ego while the Council gaped.

Jasper held up a hand and slowly the clamouring ceased. Into the silence, still sitting on a chair of truth runes, Bastion spoke. 'I'm Ellie Tron.'

There was a collective gasp of shock. No one had expected that, least of all me. Did Bastion have some sort of immunity to truth runes? But that was unheard of...

He elaborated. 'I'm an observant man and over the centuries I've learned a great deal about runing. It is easy to acquire the right potions for the right price, and I am a wealthy man. I have killed hundreds in my life, thousands even. I am keen to atone for the blood on my hands.'

Though all he was saying was true, he was wordsmithing for all he was worth. But that didn't change the fact that he'd said he was Ellie Tron. How had he done that while under the power of the truth runes? I had never seen anyone lie under so many of them. It shouldn't be possible. Yet here he was, lying – because *I* was Ellie Tron.

'But...' Seren spluttered. 'You're not a witch!'

Bastion shrugged nonchalantly. 'Non-witches can use runes and potions as much as a witch can. Of course the spell-work is nowhere near as effective but it *can* work. I am a griffin. Your "charging for healing" policy does not apply to me.'

The stunned silence in the room was deafening until Kass broke it. 'All in favour of dropping the charges against Amber DeLea?'

I heard a handful of muttered 'ayes'.

'I want your word that the charges levelled here today against Amber will never be repeated,' Bastion continued. 'Someone is trying to smear her good name and that stops now.'

'I agree,' Kass said quickly. 'And I also agree that no charges will be levelled against you, Bastion, as you are not under purview of our laws. Is the Council in agreement?'

There was another round of 'ayes'.

'Release Miss DeLea!' Kass called.

Bastion stood up and left the sphere of the truth runes. Before he could reach me, Mack stepped forward, his eyes blazing with hatred. The moment hummed with tension and I wondered for a moment if he was planning to use the

IR against me. Instead he released me from my cuffs with a malevolent glare.

Magic returned to me with such force that I swayed on my feet. Bastion was there, wrapping a steadying arm around my waist. 'Easy, Bambi,' he murmured. 'I've got you.'

I forced myself to nod, to swallow down the hundred questions swirling in my brain. He'd done it; he'd gotten me off all the charges and I hadn't even been questioned with the truth runes. The burning question was ... how?

Chapter 8

I gave Benji another hug. He had decided that he wanted to stay in Edinburgh to teach David the ropes; I suspected that he didn't want David to feel as lonely as he had done. It was incredibly kind so, although I'd miss him, I didn't argue with his decision. Benji deserved the chance to make up his own mind, be the master of his fate – as much as he could be with the Council's claws dug firmly into his soul.

He hugged me back gently. 'I'll miss you, Am Bam,' he whispered.

I smiled. 'You'll be so busy making friends you won't have time to miss me. If you need me, call. You've got a phone now.' Bastion had given Benji one of his burner phones and put in his own, Oscar's and my numbers. We were only a call away if he needed us.

'I will, Am.'

'Be careful of black witches,' I pleaded. 'No heroics. If you see anything suspicious, let me know. I'll deal with them.' Or, more likely, Bastion would.

Benji nodded, eyes serious. 'I will,' he promised again.

I slid into the back of the car with Bastion close behind me. Oscar started the engine and we moved off. Now we were alone, I could demand some answers. As I turned to him, Bastion held up one finger. He rooted around in his backpack then pulled out a small handheld device, turned it on and started waving it around the inside of the car.

'You're checking for bugs,' I surmised.

He nodded then switched off the device and put it back in his backpack. 'We're good.' He was still eyeing the shadows in the car intently. 'How do you feel about Frogmatch?' he asked. 'Do you trust him?'

'As much as I trust anyone, I guess. He's definitely helped us a lot these last few days.'

Bastion settled back in his seat. 'Tell me about the vampyr.'

'Not much to tell. It turns out my father is a necromancer and he sent a vampyr to have a tête-à-tête with me. I killed it. End of story.' I wanted to brush aside the whole episode. 'Now, more importantly, how the hell did you lie under truth runes?'

He looked at me intently. 'I didn't.'

'Obviously you did! I'm Ellie Tron and I killed Hilary.' And now I had a vampyr to add to my list of victims; I was turning into quite the serial killer. I shoved the dark feeling down. That was the healthy way to deal with it. 'What's going on?' I asked. 'How did you lie?'

Bastion looked frustrated and exchanged a glance with Oscar.

'What's going on?' I repeated, letting my frustration with them both leak into my voice. I'm not into swearing, but at that moment cuss words were starting to feel like a good addition to my vocabulary. How had Bastion avoided the truth runes? Had he somehow built up an immunity to them?

'We can't tell you,' Bastion sighed. 'You've got to work it out for yourself. It seems obvious to me, but I guess it's different when you don't know. You have to put all of the clues together.' Obviously frustrated, he ran a hand through his hair.

Great: now I was feeling stupid on top of everything else.

'You've been stubbornly avoiding the biggest clue,' Bastion added. 'I know you hate it, Amber, but it's time to go to the Seers.'

My stomach lurched. The prophecy; the prophecy about me. The one Mum had mentioned a number of times, the one I'd been avoiding at all costs. I hated fate, hated prophecy. Dammit, I was the mistress of my own ship. 'The Hall of Prophecy,' I shifted uncomfortably at the thought.

'Not there,' Bastion disagreed. 'Melva. We need to go to Melva.'

'What? Why?'

'Because Melva never registered it.'

I started. Melva was the Seers' High Priestess and their laws are clear: they *have* to register a prophecy within three years. Melva had never struck me as a rebel. 'She never registered it? Why the heck not?'

'The prophecy paints a target on your back, Bambi. Your mum didn't want your dad getting wind of it. The prophecy was spilled just before your father ... left. If he'd learned of its existence, as your parent he could have accessed it until you were eighteen years old when it became your property.'

'You think that's one of the reasons Mum kicked him to the kerb when she did,' I stated slowly.

Bastion nodded. Great. Now I not only felt stupid, I felt guilty, too. My parents' marital breakdown could be laid at my prophecy-cursed door.

I frowned. 'The Seers are supposed to register the prophecy within three years, right? Couldn't Melva have registered it after my father disappeared?'

Bastion looked serious. 'Yes. If her omission becomes known, she could lose her position as High Priestess.'

Oh heck. Melva had risked a lot to keep me safe. As I'd done errand after errand for her over the years I'd thought that *she* owed *me*, but it turned out the scales had always been weighted in her favour. I just hadn't known it.

'Good luck getting an appointment,' Oscar grunted bitterly. 'Her secretary is a right ogre.' He paused. 'Not a real one, obviously. She actually appears to be a low-level Seer herself.'

'This is fascinating,' a little voice piped up. 'I do love a good prophecy!'

Bastion didn't move a muscle, didn't so much as blink. He'd known we'd had a stowaway from the start.

'Hello, Frogmatch,' I said to the disembodied voice, amused. 'Did you sneak into our car?'

'I did, your ladyship, I did.'

'Do you promise not to break it?' I pressed. Imps adore sabotaging cars, trains and planes. If it moves, they want to break it. The last thing we needed was a flat tyre on top of everything else.

There was a sigh. 'You ask a lot, but since destiny is calling I won't play with the electronics. It wouldn't do for you to be late for destiny. Well … lat*er*. It seems this prophecy has already been hanging about for a while, Ellie.' Frogmatch scurried out of the boot of the car and smiled at me with a mouth full of spiky teeth.

Frogmatch is eight inches tall and has vibrant red skin, which looked far brighter than it had when he'd visited me in the clinic after a vampyr had removed his tail. I'd healed the tail and saved his life; in exchange he'd given me a kiss and an offer of help. Last night I'd summoned him to my cell and an hour later he had appeared – how, I had no idea. I knew very little about imp magic: they are a secretive bunch.

I'd asked Frogmatch for his help, outlined what I needed him to do, and he'd scurried off to save my bacon. As it turned out, Bastion had also been plotting to save me in his own way, but I figured both of them had contributed to my release.

Now Frogmatch was standing before me, his forked tail curved up his body, his right hand wrapped around it as if he were reassuring himself that it was still there. His antlers were in fine fettle and he had a little white loincloth looped around his waist to preserve his modesty. Apart from the loincloth he was naked. His toenails were curved and black, like mini-claws; they were probably quite good as a defence weapon, but frankly the pocket-sized talons looked adorable.

'Prophecy is for the directionless,' I harrumphed to the imp. 'I know what I'm doing with my life.'

'If the griffin says you need to know it, then you need to know it.' Frogmatch waggled a finger at me.

I was being schooled by a creature no bigger than my hand, and the worst thing was that he was completely right. I sighed. It looked like I was going prophecy hunting.

Chapter 9

I pulled out my phone and rang Melva's private number. It was early afternoon, and I'd no doubt missed her lunch hour, so I didn't expect her to answer promptly, if at all. I was ready to leave a voice message when the call connected.

'Hello, Amber,' she said in a mysterious voice. 'I've been expecting your call.'

I rolled my eyes. 'Knock it off. You knew it was me because of caller ID.'

I heard the smile in her voice. 'That too. You're coming to see me.'

It wasn't a question but I answered it anyway. 'Yes.'

'Perfect timing. My 2pm appointment has just left and I've nothing until 4pm.' She said the last words with a weird emphasis.

'Ok-ay. We won't be there that soon because we're still in Scotland. Are you free this evening?'

'From 7pm,' she confirmed.

'Great.' I cleared my throat. 'We need to talk about my prophecy.'

'Yes. Thank the Goddess.' She sighed happily. 'The relief ... it's amazing. I've been dragging it around for years. The weight of it...'

'What?' I asked in confusion. 'How is a prophecy heavy?'

'It's metaphysically heavy. There's a reason we're supposed to record the prophecies in the Hall of Prophecy,' she explained. 'When we recite a prophecy, it clings to us. Every day that it's attached to us, it uses our strength to remain here in *this* realm, in our memories. When we place the prophecies in the orbs, their link with us dissipates and frees us. It's like constantly walking around carrying a heavy rock, then you set it down and your arms feel floaty and light. When I agreed to keep your prophecy, I had no idea it would continue to grow or how heavy it would become. I've been looking forward to this day with all my heart, even with the consequences.' She hummed happily.

'Why didn't you say anything?' I asked, aghast. 'I would have heard the prophecy sooner if I'd known what it was costing you to hold it.'

'You weren't ready to hear it and it wasn't ready to be spoken. But I'm glad that today is the day. I'll see you later, perhaps earlier than you think. And Amber?'

'Yes?'

'I regret nothing.' She hung up.

I rolled my eyes. 'Why do Seers always try to be mysterious?'

'What did she say?' Oscar asked.

'She said she'd see me later and that perhaps I'd arrive earlier than I expected. I said we'd be there for 7pm.'

'I doubt we'll get there any earlier, not with this traffic.' Oscar gestured at the slow-moving vehicles in front of us. It was going to take us a while to get from Edinburgh back to the Home Counties.

Bastion frowned. 'What?' I asked.

His expression cleared. 'Nothing.'

If I'd had Jinx's lie-detecting skills, I'm pretty sure they would just have pinged. Bastion was keeping something from me.

Chapter 10

I was relieved to see that the lights were still on in Melva's office. She had been totally wrong: we were actually later than we'd expected and it was nearly 8pm. The traffic gods had not been kind.

'Are you coming in?' I asked Oscar. He often stayed in the car, ready to make a quick getaway, but the prophecy felt like a big deal and I'd rather he knew it – if he didn't already. I often talked over big things with Oscar and this felt like it was going to be a doozy.

He hesitated. 'I'd like to come in, if you don't mind me hearing the prophecy.'

'You don't know it?' I asked, a little surprised. Mum had bound Oscar and Bastion in knots with oaths and I knew they were keeping a cluster of secrets from me, so I'd assumed that they both already knew the prophecy. You know what they say about *ass*-umptions; now I was the donkey.

Oscar shook his head. 'Not the full thing, just roughly what it says.'

'And you?' I asked Bastion.

He also shook his head. 'Not the full wording. I'd like to hear it as well.'

'I'll come,' Frogmatch offered. 'I'll guard you all while you hear it. I don't need to hear it – I already know you're destined for greatness.'

My heart warmed at his gallant offer. The idea of him guarding Bastion was kind of laughable but I kept my face straight. 'That's very kind of you, but you've already helped me a great deal. My treatment of you that day was free. You didn't need to give me your kiss or your name, but I used them and called you. If there was ever any debt between us, it is certainly gone now. Our balance sheet is wiped clean.'

Frogmatch shook his head solemnly. 'My Ellie-lady, it will never be wiped out. You helped me, then you helped Brambleford and you saved both our lives. We discussed it and agreed that my indentured servitude to you was the way forward.'

How generous of Brambleford, I thought drily. 'Absolutely not! I have no desire to have a slave, Frogmatch. Besides, there is *no* debt to pay off. None.'

He smiled. 'And *that* is why there is. You're a good person, Ellie. I'm going to help you achieve something amazing. They'll sing songs about Ellie and Frogmatch one day.'

'I'm not. I won't. I'm just an ordinary witch,' I said, suddenly weary.

He snorted. 'There's nothing ordinary about you, sweet cheeks. You can accept my offer and provide me with accommodation and food, or I'll follow you around homeless for the rest of my days.' He shrugged like he was indifferent to my decision.

'You are absolutely not being homeless on my account,' I huffed, folding my arms.

'Good! Then we are agreed. I'll live with you and guard you with my life. Done and done. So mote it be.' He stamped his right foot and his black claws clacked on the leather seats. His skin flashed with a bright light before settling back to its usual red colour.

My mouth dropped open again. He had sworn a magical oath. Damn it.

Bastion was smiling. 'Nice,' he commented. He held out his hand to Frogmatch and they shared a fist bump. Frogmatch winked at Bastion and Bastion's smile widened. Oh goody, my bodyguards were bonding. Wonderful.

I opened the car door. Whoever damn well wanted to hear the prophecy could come with me – the more the merrier. All three men were sworn to protect me, so it made sense that they should learn what they were fighting against. Maybe Frogmatch would change his mind and we could work out a way to release him from his hasty little oath. This was a mess.

And, aside from the prophecy, I still had a tonne of work to do. Every spare moment I'd had I had been working on finding a mate for Krieg, plus I'd started making the final-defence potion for Shirdal and Bastion. Then there was my mum's CD to open. Some days, it felt like I should have just stayed in bed.

I pushed open the front door to Melva's office and felt oddly disappointed that her bitchy secretary Nell wasn't there. She was a nightmare to deal with but I enjoyed getting one over her, and our bitchy banter always made me grin secretly. Still, it was one less obstacle to getting inside.

I knew where Melva's office was located, so I pushed past the secretary's desk to the stairway behind it. Bastion and Oscar followed me with Frogmatch riding on Oscar's shoulder, looking for all the world like the daemon side of someone's conscience.

I took the stairs two at a time. Melva's door was slightly ajar and I pushed it open. 'Hi! I told you we wouldn't be...'

I trailed off, eyes widening in horror. Melva was sitting at her desk, her eyes open but unseeing. There were no signs of violence but she was motionless. I stared, dumfounded, waiting for her chest to rise. It didn't.

I swallowed hard. There could be no doubt: Melva was dead.

For once, I let an expletive come to mind.

Fuck.

Chapter 11

Inspector Stacy Wise studied me with her green eyes. 'You definitely didn't move the body?' she asked evenly.

I shook my head. 'No. It was obvious that Melva was dead. We didn't touch her at all – there was nothing to be done.'

Frogmatch had made himself scarce before the Connection Inspector arrived. 'I'm allergic to the Man,' he'd explained. 'I'll be around, Ellie, don't you worry. I'll always find you.' With that slightly sinister promise, he'd scurried into the bookshelf behind Melva's body and disappeared from sight. I couldn't help keeping an eye out for him but I hadn't seen so much as a flicker of his pronged tail.

'Why were you visiting her so late?' Wise asked, notepad ready to jot down my response.

I gave a one-shouldered shrug, 'We were going to have a cup of tea and a catch up,' I lied smoothly.

'I didn't know you were friends with Mel.' Her eyes were cynical; she wasn't buying it.

The best defence is a good offence, so I went on the attack. 'Were you friends?' I demanded.

She folded her arms. 'Yes, as it happens.'

'Then isn't it a conflict of interest for you investigate her death?'

Wise shook her head sharply. 'No. I'm highly motivated to find her killers.'

'You'll be emotional.' I kept my voice even. 'You'll make mistakes.'

'Did you make a mistake when you located the Crone's killer?' Wise batted back.

I tried hard not to react. Hilary's death hadn't been officially notified to the Connection, so that meant that Wise had an informant in the Covens.

'Besides,' she raised an eyebrow, 'do you see me sobbing?'

I looked at Bastion. 'Toxic toughness. She might need a tear-jerker movie, too,' I murmured in an aside to him. His lips curved up in response.

Wise glared. She'd heard my whisper. Oops.

'I'm a woman,' she snapped. 'If one tear rolls down my cheek when I'm on the job, my colleagues say I'm on my period or that I'm "just" an emotional woman. Most women in most work places have to work ten times as hard to be taken as seriously as their male counterparts. And yes, in this day and age there is *still* a pay disparity, even in the Inspectors' wages. Do you know how many female Inspectors there are in the UK? Ten. That's it.

'You're a witch. Although there are male witches too, you've been raised in a largely matriarchal system. You honour the Coven mothers and the Triune – and there are no Coven *fathers*. But for the rest of us? The glass ceiling is still there and I refuse to enforce it by letting one iota of emotion show while I'm working.' She glared. 'That doesn't mean I'm dead inside.'

She said that with the same force I used when I protested that, even though I didn't have a familiar, I still had a soul. Clearly it was a common refrain.

I blinked at her vehemence; I'd obviously hit a nerve. I didn't point out that she was letting her emotions show at that moment – she was brimming with anger, and anger is one of the stages of grief. We don't all trot through the stages of grief in the same order; personally, I was still snuggling down with denial.

I cleared my throat awkwardly. 'Of course not. Bastion pointed out to me that I have difficulty in crying. It's a "me" problem. I didn't mean to offend you.' Sometimes I wasn't the most sensitive soul but I was working hard on getting better.

'I can cry,' Wise muttered a shade sulkily. 'But I don't – not on the job.'

'Sure. That's fine.'

She glared. 'Thank you for your acceptance of how I deal with my emotions.' Her tone was heavy with sarcasm.

When we'd met in Liverpool she'd seemed nicer but I guessed standing over the corpse of your friend would make anyone crabby.

I looked at Melva's body and sighed. Of course I was sorry she was dead – she'd been a nice woman and a well-respected Seer – but I'd fibbed to Wise. We hadn't been friends, though we had respected each other and worked well together for a couple of decades. Before Jinx, Lucy and Bastion had wormed their way into my heart, she'd probably been the closest thing to a friend that I'd had. Certainly I'd considered her a colleague, or perhaps more an equal since she was a Seer to my witch. Still, I could admit to myself that I would miss her.

And worse, now that Melva was dead the prophecy had died with her.

Chapter 12

We spent a further half an hour with Wise, each of us giving a brief statement about what we'd seen – all of which amounted to three statements that said little. We hung around long enough for the crime-scene investigation team to arrive and then Wise cut us loose.

'I'll be in touch after the forensic pathologist has examined the body and has an idea of cause of death.' She offered the olive branch grudgingly, but she was a smart woman and she knew she needed connections and allies to get ahead.

I took the same approach: powerful associates are helpful. 'Thank you, I'd appreciate that,' I said as warmly as I could, which was a shade above glacial.

She nodded briskly and turned back to managing the scene. We returned to the car. Frogmatch's absence worried me. Would he follow us out or would he wreak havoc with Wise's crime scene? I looked around but I couldn't see him.

Reluctantly, I slid into the car without him. 'Well,' I said as I shut the door, 'that's made things a lot more difficult.' I sighed, rubbing my tired eyes. Someone else had to know the prophecy. 'Who else knows the prophecy besides Melva?' I asked the men.

'Your mum heard it,' Oscar pointed out. 'But it could be weeks before she's ... present again. And even then, there's every possibility she will mis-remember a word or phrase. You can't afford that.'

Frogmatch popped up from the boot again, making me start in surprise. 'Goddess! You startled me!' I protested.

Bastion didn't so much as blink. He was aware of his surroundings in a way I would never be. Once more, he'd known that Frogmatch was there; I was glad that one of us had.

'I saw something surprising,' Frogmatch said, looking at me oddly.

'What?' I asked impatiently.

'You.'

'How is that surprising?' I raised an eyebrow.

'There were two of you.'

Oscar thunked his head on the steering wheel and let out a low groan. 'I guess we know where we're going next.' He sighed.

'Indeed,' Bastion murmured.

I looked at them. Two of me at one time only meant one thing – time travel.

Hellhounds can manipulate the realms, including the Third realm that allows you to influence time. Jinx's bonded hellhound, Gato, was off on honeymoon with her and Emory.

'Gato isn't accessible right now.' I pointed out. Indy had been left at home with Tom Smith, but she was a pup; I wasn't sure I'd trust her to shove me through time when she could barely restrain any of her baser urges. She'd destroyed Emory's shoes. A lot of them.

'We don't need a hellhound,' Oscar confirmed grimly.

I frowned. The only alternative to a hellhound was a temporal portal. There was only one in the whole of the UK. Surely he couldn't mean that?

'The temporal portal in St Luke's is heavily guarded,' I pointed out. 'Prohibitively so. Besides, we've just driven all the way from Scotland. You can't seriously want to turn around and drive all the way to Liverpool right now?

'Want to? No,' Oscar confirmed. 'But do we need to? It looks like it. If Frogmatch saw two of you, then it's time for some temporal surfing.'

'Sneaking in past the portal's wizard guards will be virtually impossible,' I argued. 'That means we need permission from the Symposium and the only Symposium member who might vote to let us in is Kass. And as the newest member, I doubt she's even been to a Symposium meeting yet. She'll have zero clout to get the others to agree.'

'We don't need *her* clout,' Bastion said. 'We have Oscar's.'

'What has Oscar got to do with anything?' I frowned. I hated how Bastion seemed to know more about Oscar than me, even though Oscar had virtually raised me and was my father in all but name.

Oscar met my gaze in the rear-view mirror. 'You know that I worked for the Connection before I formally joined the Coven as Luna's bodyguard.'

'Yes...'

'I worked as a temporal guard.'

My mouth dropped open. 'What?' Temporal guards are reputed to be hardened killers, former black-operators doing a slightly cushier job before retirement came their way. Being a temporal guard is physically demanding and only the operatives at the top of their game are invited to become one. They retain the position for a year or two, then the cream of the next crop replaces them.

From waking Oscar abruptly a time or two I knew that he'd been a dangerous man at some point in his life – that he still was. Even so, I still found it hard to reconcile that knowledge with the image of the man who put overnight oats and fresh orange juice in my fridge.

Oscar went on, 'For seven years.'

Seven years? 'That's unheard of.'

'He's something of a legend,' Bastion confirmed. 'Think Rambo but guarding the bombed-out church instead.'

I wondered whether Mum had known what Oscar had done for a living before she hired him. Suddenly everything clicked into place. Of course she had; Oscar and Mum had dated *before* he'd become her bodyguard. He'd only agreed to be her driver and guard on condition that their relationship was noted – and permitted – under the contract of employment.

I stared at Oscar dumbly and he grimaced as I finally connected the dots. Mum had worked several jobs to make ends meet, yet she'd been present during my childhood.

She'd raised me and been mother and father to me until Oscar had stepped into the latter role. 'You let her use the portal,' I whispered.

'You've met your mother, haven't you?' he demanded. 'There was no "letting" her, not once she'd got her claws into my heart. She said it was essential, that there had been a prophecy... I shouldn't have done it, but I did. There isn't a day goes by that I don't regret it.'

My jaw dropped. 'Are you seriously saying that she used the portal to do ... what?'

Oscar grimaced again. 'I can't tell you why she used the portal. You try saying no to your mother. She's a force of nature.'

'She *was*,' I agreed harshly. 'Goddess ... her dementia. It's not dementia at all, is it? It's temporal displacement.' I didn't even try to keep the fury out of my voice. 'It's your fault she's like this,' my voice whipped out.

I was feeling the sharp sting of betrayal, never mind that the betrayal had been carried out three decades earlier. I didn't have my mum *now* and it was Oscar's fault. It wasn't just a heinous disease ravaging her but something more: a conscious choice on her part. She had chosen to raise me back then knowing that she would be leaving me *now*. It was a bitter pill to swallow – and Oscar had enabled it. Oh, he and Bastion were right – of course they were. Mum was a difficult woman to say no to, but I didn't have her to rail at right now so Oscar would have to do.

'Amber—' Bastion said softly.

'No,' Oscar interrupted. 'She's right. It kills me, but she's right.'

'Luna made her decision. She knew what it would cost her,' Bastion disagreed firmly. 'I warned her at the time. She is responsible for her own actions. She always was.'

'Oscar enabled her actions,' I spat. Bastion grimaced but had nothing to rebut that.

My world was imploding. I was angry not just with Oscar but with Mum. She'd meddled with time and lost her mind, and she had done it willingly. I suffered every day in her absence and she had chosen it.

And worse – I was about to do the same thing.

Chapter 13

'Without a hellhound bond protecting my mind, if we go back in time I'll end up like Mum with more holes in my memory than a Swiss-cheese slice,' I asserted grimly.

Bastion shook his head. 'It's time *abuse* that causes the phenomenon, not simply one or two trips. No one knows exactly how many trips it will take for your brain to be affected – more than three, certainly. Once the Connection learned about the issue, they tested extensively. Different subjects survived with their minds intact with different degrees of exposure, and four trips was the minimum number where a negative affect was recorded. Soon after that, the Symposium re-shuffled its members. The new members were aghast at the immorality of testing on their employees and shut the programme down.' He raised an eyebrow at me. 'Have you been back in time before?'

I shook my head. 'Not properly. I've used my watch to slow time.'

'Then we'll be fine,' he said with a shrug.

Oscar cleared his throat. 'I've had my three times, so you'll be going without me.' He looked at me compassionately. 'I still think you need one parental figure in your life, and I don't want to join Luna and leave you bereft.'

Mad as I was at Oscar, I gave him a tight nod. He was right: the thought of losing him... No way in heck was he going through the portal a fourth time.

'I can get you into the portal, though,' he promised.

'Fine,' I said shortly. I couldn't bring myself to be warmer than that, but I wasn't shouting at him so he'd have to take that as a win.

'I only saw you two – Ellie and Bastion – so I'd better stay in this time as well,' Frogmatch grumbled, looking downcast. He'd want to cause mayhem so I had no doubt that it was in everyone's best interests that he stayed right here. One Frogmatch wandering about felt like more than enough.

'Just you and me, Bambi.' Bastion smiled. 'I guess it's a date.' He was trying to distract me from my emotions and I let him.

'And you bitched about Emory taking Jinx to the Kelpies for a date?' I teased archly.

'I do a lot of things better than Emory,' Bastion smirked.

'Including dates and having a big head?'

He grinned. 'It's only big-headed if it's not true.'

'So for our first date you're taking me to meet a Seer,' I said flatly. 'Romantic.'

'No, for our first date I'm taking you to embrace your destiny.' He winked.

'Smooth,' I complimented him drily.

He sobered, moved closer to me and gently cupped my chin, turning my head so I met his dark eyes. 'This isn't really a date, Bambi. I want to be clear on that. When I take you out for the first time, we're going to do something special. Just us.' His voice lowered. 'And you're going to love every minute of it.'

My heart was thundering in my chest and suddenly my mouth was dry. I licked my lips. 'That's a bold claim,' I managed to reply evenly, like my knees weren't weak at the thought of 'loving every minute' of being with Bastion.

'I'm a bold man. I don't do things by halves, Amber. When I'm in, I'm all in.'

Now there was a promise. The question was, was I ready to be *all in* with Bastion?

Chapter 14

The bombed-out church was more heavily guarded than usual. Not too long ago, a rogue Seer had tried to seize control of the portal to subvert it for her own use. Not unlike how my mother had *actually* used it, apparently.

Unlike Mum, the Seer had wanted to wrest control of the Connection from the Symposium and start her own ruling dynasty. She had hired an army of ogres and trolls and cut her way to the portal. As a result of that incident, the bombed-out church was crawling with wizards ready to kill people who wanted to use the portal without the appropriate Symposium authorisation. We just had to wade through them. Easy.

We'd driven for hours to get to Liverpool. It was knocking on midnight, my butt was numb, my temper was short and I was tired and cranky. I was also incredibly nervous.

It wasn't every day that I broke into a heavily guarded government building.

'How are we doing this?' I asked, crouched next to a bush and feeling ridiculous – I am no GI Jane. I had my ever-present tote bag slung over my shoulder, packed with healing potions and an illusion potion.

I would admit to no one that I was hoping that I'd somehow be able to save Melva. I had helped Jinx pull off a miracle a time or two, and I hoped that Melva had a miracle coming her way. Maybe the body I'd seen had been an illusion painted on another corpse. I hadn't seen the illusion break while we were there with Wise, but it was still possible even if it didn't feel probable.

'The portal is held in what used to be the nave of the church. There's a hidden entrance for employees to the side of it that is accessible in emergencies,' Oscar explained.

'And you still have a key?' I asked hopefully.

'No, but I know the code.'

I stared. 'That's your plan? Use an old code? Oscar! They will have changed that code a decade ago!'

'It's a master code. Different codes are generated every day, but there's only one master code. In the whole time I worked there, they never changed it.'

'And you're hoping they still won't have?' I asked incredulously.

'If it doesn't work, we go to Plan B. But people are creatures of habit – the code will be the same,' Oscar said confidently.

'What's Plan B?'

'Fire and bombs.' Bastion grinned. 'Maybe even a Molotov cocktail or two.' He sounded rather excited about the prospect. Someone was gunning for Plan B.

I pinched the bridge of my nose. *Goddess, let Plan A work,* I prayed. It was just too late in the evening for bombs; they were more of an early morning thing.

'I'm going to make it so we can't be seen,' Oscar murmured.

I blinked. 'I thought you couldn't use the IR on yourself.'

'I can't. I'm using the IR on anyone that we encounter. Interestingly, it works on CCTV footage as well. Jinx mentioned that once.'

'Huh.' I thought about it. 'We'll need to be visible when we go into the past. Frogmatch saw us.'

'You will be,' Oscar promised. 'I won't have cast the spell on you in the past.'

The whole thing made my head hurt. Bastion laced our fingers together, so we'd be in contact even if we were invisible. 'Do it,' he ordered Oscar.

A moment later, we winked out of sight. I lifted our joined hands but, although I could feel Bastion's warm skin, I couldn't see a damned thing. It was disconcerting.

Bastion tugged me up and I took a step forward. It was horrible not being able to see my feet; the foliage was tamped down where I was standing but I was invisible. I felt ethereal and ghostly and I didn't like it one bit. I hoped it wasn't a sign of what was to come.

We walked forward until we came to a door and a code box. It beeped as Oscar put in the code and I held my breath while we waited to see if it worked or if Plan B – B for bomb – would be needed.

The light flashed green then the door gave an obnoxiously loud buzz and popped open. It opened further and I hoped Oscar was pulling it rather than a guard who was curious about what appeared to be a self-opening door.

Bastion and I waited a beat. When there were no cries of alarm, he tugged me forward. My heart was thudding, and not in a Bastion-is-looking-at-me-like-I'm-cake kind of a way, and my palms were sweaty. I'm good in a crisis when blood is on the floor, but it seemed that creeping in darkness to break into a forbidden portal was not in my skillset.

Frankly, I was peeing myself. I wished I could blame early menopause but I wasn't there yet; it was just me being cowardly. *Not cowardly,* I told myself firmly. Cowardly would be if I'd stayed home with a hot drink and a good book. Instead I was terrified but still moving forward, one step at a time. *You're facing your fear, DeLea,* I told myself, *and that's brave. Keep stepping forward.*

Luckily, Bastion was skilled in this sort of ninja crap. He led us onwards, pausing occasionally. We made achingly slow progress as we passed a number of guards. I felt sure that they could hear the hammering of my heart; I was certain it was breaking the silence around me.

The soldiers we passed were focused on their job. There was no idle chatter or hint of comradeship. They were alert and ready. Unfortunately for us.

We continued to sneak so slowly that it felt like we might be going backwards. Every time I glanced at the portal, it was still so damned far away but finally, after what felt like several days, we were near it. One guard was standing directly in front of it.

Bastion tugged my hand to make me crouch down as we watched the guard. He didn't move; he didn't so much as shift his weight. He was directly in our path, and I had no idea how we'd get around him short of tugging him into the portal with us. Which would mean we took one helluva pissed-off soldier back in time with us. I couldn't think of another option, though; we couldn't crouch there forever waiting for the changing of the guard. And every second that passed made it more likely we would be found.

'Unless you want me to slice his throat, you'll need to use a sleep potion on him,' Bastion whispered so quietly I had to strain to hear him. 'It'll take too long to choke him and the other guards will be on us in a flash. We need something that's almost instant.'

I baulked at the idea of painting an anaesthetic potion with an *isa* rune on someone who was unaware of it, but the thought of Bastion killing a man who was only doing his job pleased me even less. I guessed the sleep potion was the only other option.

I moved Bastion's hand to my shoulder and pulled my tote bag around to the front of my body. I slowly un-did the zip and the faint sound made me wince, but the guard didn't look in our direction once. Opening my bag as silently as I could, I pulled out a jar.

Thankfully everything about me seemed to be invisible including my clothes *and* my potions, so the guard wasn't confronted by a jar floating through the air. Unfortunately, because everything on me was invisible including my clothes *and* my potions, I couldn't tell by touch which Kilner jar was which.

I fumbled around until I found a metal clasp, carefully opened the lid and sniffed. Ach! The acrid scent told me it was a healing potion. I closed the lid carefully and set it down by my foot so that I could return it to my bag after I'd located the correct jar.

It was like some kind of crazy lucky dip. I grabbed another jar and tried again. The familiar scent of an anaesthetic potion wafted up to me. Thank the Goddess; I had ten jars of potions with me so I was lucky to have found the right one so quickly.

I rifled through my bag to find my favourite paintbrush, which I could recognise by its width and the feel of its wooden handle. I dipped it into the pot and scooped up a generous amount of potion, then closed the pot and put it back in my bag. I picked up the potion by my foot and stowed that away, too. Then I slung my bag round to my back and stepped forward.

Bastion followed me, keeping his hand firmly on my shoulder. His touch reassured me; I was certainly playing in amateur hour but he wasn't. He did this kind of thing all the time and he had my back.

I approached the guard from the side. The bombed-out church was lit with fairy lights, adding a soft glow to the darkness. The only visible skin to work with was on the back of the guard's hand or on his face. Grimacing, I aimed for the former. He'd feel the cold, slimy potion the instant it touched his skin, so I pulled my magic forward ready to activate the rune the moment it was formed. The only problem was, I couldn't see the rune I was drawing. There were definite downsides to invisibility.

It's just like any other runing, I told myself firmly.

My heart was still hammering in my ears as I reached forward and drew *isa* on the back of the guard's hand in two quick strokes. He frowned and looking down then raised his other hand, no doubt to wipe at the wet sensation. I released my magic through the rune before he could make contact with it. In my urgency, I used a little too much magic and he collapsed instantly in a dead faint.

Presumably Bastion or Oscar caught him at the last moment because invisible hands lowered him gently to the ground.

'Go!' Oscar hissed. 'Picture the time and the location you need, then walk through the portal!'

'Three pm, Melva's offices,' Bastion murmured to me. His hand slid down my shoulder to find my fingers again and his breath tickled my ear, doing all sorts of interesting things to my body. I had no time to examine them further or to respond as he tugged me forward. Hands linked once more, we walked forward into the shimmering light and let the portal consume us.

Three pm, Melva's offices.

Chapter 15

We'd stepped into the portal in darkness but it spat us out into light. As Oscar had predicted, his IR magic had been stripped from us and suddenly I could see Bastion holding my hand. It made my tummy give a happy lurch to see my pale skin next to his tanned flesh. His skin was rougher than mine, like he'd seen hard work. My hands had too, but I moisturise compulsively. It is my one vanity.

I was ogling Bastion whilst he was looking around and checking for danger. Seeing none he relaxed slightly, but only a fool would have thought he wasn't ready to eviscerate them at any time. Our little jaunt into invisibility was a reminder that not all our enemies would be so obliging as to be visible and announce their arrival with trumpets.

Bastion had tucked his body around me defensively. I'd like to have pretended it was because he wanted to hug me, but I knew it was so that he could be my griffin-shield. I looked up at the exact moment that he looked down at me. His eyes were dark and focused on me with an intensity I rarely saw. They flicked to my lips and I was suddenly sure that this was going to be the moment of our first kiss. My body swayed a little closer of its own volition.

Tension hummed between us, but Bastion didn't make his move. I looked at him, lust fading to confusion. Did he want me to make a move instead? Worse – what if he didn't want me at all? Uncertainty and anxiety lanced through me.

He reached down and lifted my chin up so our eyes met. 'I want you, Bambi, more than you know,' he admitted ruefully. 'But not yet. Not until you know.'

'Know what?' I asked desperately.

'The truth.' He stepped away from me and the distance between us suddenly felt like a chasm. Secrets again. I hate secrets.

I took a moment to steady myself. We weren't here for Bastion and me to kiss. We had travelled through time for an important reason and everything else would have to wait. If I wasn't going to be kissed then I'd better damn well save someone's life instead.

I started up the stairs to Melva's office with Bastion hot on my heels. Melva's assistant Nell glared at me as I walked in. 'She can't just fit you in!' she started before I could open my mouth.

'That's not true, Nell, is it? Melva already told me she has a three o'clock slot free for me. Buzz her. Now.' I gave her my best death glare.

Nell hesitated; she clearly didn't want to do what I'd demanded but she knew I was right about the time slot and she didn't want to disobey Melva's wishes. 'She's had a busy day – she spent all morning consulting for the vampyrs. She's tired. Keep it short,' she ordered.

'Are you her secretary or her nurse?' I bit back.

'Her friend – an alien concept to you, I'm sure.'

Ouch, that was a direct hit. But she was wrong; I was, at the ripe age of over forty, finally getting to grips with this friendship thing. I could count the number of friends I had on one hand – though only just: Jinx, Lucy, Bastion, Benji and Kass. That was a huge achievement for me and I wasn't going to let Nell or anyone else make me feel bad about it.

Nell buzzed Melva. When she got the all clear, she sent us into her boss's office with a glare.

Melva smiled brightly at us as we walked in. 'Amber!' She stood to greet us. 'Bastion! What a pleasure. Nell seemed to think you'd already made an appointment and

I didn't disabuse her of the notion.' She gave a little bow and looked at us curiously. 'How did you know I was free?'

'You told us,' I said bluntly, too tired to skirt around the subject. It had been the middle of the night when we'd stepped through the portal. Even though the sun was still shining here, my body wasn't fooled. It was tired as heck.

'Did I?' She raised an eyebrow and nodded, like she'd decided something. 'My time is nigh, then.'

Her words made my scalp prickle. She knew of her impending death. I shook my head. 'Not if I can help it,' I ground out.

'Ah, Amber.' She looked at me with real sympathy. 'You cannot stop fate any more than I can. We are but bystanders in its intricate dance.'

'I don't believe that,' I snarled. 'All of us have choices. At every fork of the road we can go left or right. A thousand destinies stretch before us. Nothing is immutable. I can still save you.'

At that moment her phone rang. She looked down at it and then at me. 'It's you,' she said. 'How curious.' She swiped to answer. 'Hello, Amber,' she said, looking directly at me. 'I've been expecting your call.'

I couldn't hear my response but I didn't need to. I'd told her to knock it off and I winced a little at how rude and brash that seemed now. I'd made a quip about caller ID.

Melva grinned as she replied. 'That too. You're coming to see me.' Her eyes were laughing as she looked at me. 'Perfect timing, my 2pm appointment has just left. I've nothing on until 4pm.' She was giving me the time slot so I'd know when I needed to appear back in time.

We chatted on about my prophecy. As the phone conversation wound up, her eyes found mine again. 'You weren't ready to hear it and it wasn't ready to be said,' she said even as she studied me. 'I am glad that today is the day, though. I'll see you later – and perhaps earlier than you think. And Amber? I regret nothing.'

She hung up, eyes still locked on mine. She might regret nothing, but I was suddenly full of sorrow. I didn't want this woman to die. We might not be friends, but we were *something*. Between Bastion and I there was nothing we couldn't do, and I was determined that Melva would be breathing at the end of the day.

Chapter 16

'Can you tell me about the prophecy?' I asked abruptly.

'You're not even going to wine me and dine me first?' Melva tittered. At my flat look, she laughed even more. 'Sorry, Amber, I don't mean to tease you but you're such fun to play with.'

'Like a kitten with her fur stroked the wrong way, and she's spitting fury at you but she's only five pounds wet,' Bastion murmured, looking at me affectionately.

'Miaow,' Melva said, before laughing again.

I put my hands on my hips and glowered at them, but my heart wasn't in it. I was being teased in a friendly way; this wasn't the bitchy bullying of my childhood but a gentle prod. They were laughing *with* me rather than *at* me – well, they would be if I were laughing. 'If you two clowns are quite done,' I harrumphed, 'we have some urgent business and time is rather of the essence.'

Melva sobered. 'Talking of circuses, you'll need tell him about yours before long.' She nodded at Bastion.

Bastion stared at me. 'You have a circus?'

'Later,' I said. 'Let's focus on saving Melva for now.'

Melva breathed a soft sigh. 'Is it so soon? Tonight?'

Crud. 'You don't know exactly when?'

'I knew it would be the day I revealed the prophecy to you, and here we are.' She folded her hands in her lap.

I frowned. 'Okay, well don't reveal the prophecy to me then. We can find it out some other way then you get to live.'

Melva looked at me and her eyes were too knowing. 'For someone who doesn't believe in fate, you're awfully willing to bend to it if it means saving my life. I appreciate that, Amber, I really do. But you need to know the prophecy and you need to face it. It's already nibbling at you but you're in denial. The knowledge has been tickling your brain but you've refused to accept it. The prophecy isn't the driving force in your life, but it is going to be a tool to awaken your potential. Are you ready?'

I shook my head, stomach roiling. 'No,' I blurted out. 'I'm not.'

Bastion squeezed my hand. 'You're not alone. You're ready. *We* are ready.' His gaze told me he was giving me another clue, but whatever it was I missed it.

I blew out a sharp breath and nodded grudgingly as my fingers tightened on his. 'Hit me.'

Melva's purple skin seemed to glow with a faint luminosity and her eyes leached to purple. Her grey hair flew behind her, like it was being blown by an invisible breeze. She opened her mouth, and when the words came out they were deeper somehow, thick with portent. My neck prickled.

'Through the veils of time, a mother's plight
Her mind is the cost to set things right.
She weaves the threads of fate so tight
Her sacrifice made in love's pure light.

A griffin's wings upon the loyal guide,
A familiar bond, forever tied.
A bond hidden as the fates decide,
Loneliness consume, until realms collide.

The witch, the Crone, her destiny clear,
Black witches tremble when she's near.
With heart and rune, she'll persevere,

A hunt for justice, she'll have no peer.

But lurking deep within the night,
The Coven's head, her father's might.
A reckoning awaits in close sight
A clash of dark and radiant light.

So heed the hidden prophecy spun
Of time, protectors and battles won.
The Crone shall rise like the morning sun
To face her father, his darkness undone.'
Melva's head sank to her chest as the prophecy ended, and my head spun with the weight of the words that had fallen from her.

Chapter 17

There was so much to unpack that my brain could barely process it all. My ears were buzzing and I felt myself sliding to the floor.

My mum ... her dementia ... all of it emanating from this damned prophecy. Whatever she'd done, whatever wrongs she had righted, it had all come from her hearing this cursed thing. And so many other things had snapped into focus.

I looked for Bastion and found him kneeling before me, concern lining his face. I recited the lines that spoke of him: "'A griffin's wings upon the loyal guide, a familiar bond, forever tied. A bond hidden as the fates decide, loneliness consume, until realms collide...'"

I had spent so long perfecting a potion to find my familiar but when I'd finally drunk it, I'd learned that I already had one. I swallowed hard. 'Bastion – you're my familiar.'

I expected the words to come out as an accusation but my voice was flat. I felt numb.

'Yes,' he said simply.

So much became clear and Melva was right – I *had* known the answer but I had been wilfully ignoring it. There was only one way that Bastion could sit on so many truth runes and claim that he had killed Hilary, and that was if he were my familiar. In witch law, a witch and their familiar are seen as one entity. That was how he could successfully claim he was Ellie Tron under a truth rune. Under witch law, *he was.*

Bastion was my familiar. That was how he'd helped me recover in hospital after Becky's poisoning and the bomb. He'd used our bond to send me energy, draining himself to save me. I'd seen Lucille do that countless times to help Mum. That was why he'd gone into a restorative coma – because he'd used our bond to save me.

Bastion was my familiar. I wondered how many times I'd have to say it before it sunk in.

'The rune on your groin...' I started.

'Painted by your mother to hide the bond.'

'From whom?'

'From you.'

'Why?' I whispered brokenly, thinking of the hundreds of slights and insults I'd borne because of my lack of a familiar. From a young age it had set me apart, isolated me. 'Why?' I asked again, desperate to understand.

'A bond to a magical creature, Amber? It would have set you apart as much as having no bond did – in fact, it would have been even worse. You know the prejudice that still exists against the creatures in our world. You were so young, too young to face that prejudice. It wasn't fair to ask it of you.'

'It was *my* choice.' Rage swirled through me. My mum and Bastion had kept so much from me; they had kept *him* from me.

Bastion shook his head. 'No. You were seven. It was your parents' choice – your mother's choice. You were too young to make an informed decision.'

His eyes grew distant. 'You had a nightmare one night when I was talking with your mother. You padded in with a stuffed cat in one hand and a blanket in the other. You'd dreamed the black witches were coming to get you. You were so upset. You couldn't stop crying.'

He shook his head as if it to clear it. 'Your mum went to get you a sleep potion to settle you and you came to me. I looked at your tear-streaked face and something happened to me. You were so defenceless and scared that I promised you out loud that the black witches wouldn't get you. I meant it with all my heart. You smiled and hugged me then you went to sleep. When your mum came back, we were both glowing golden and it was too late. The bond had set.'

It was hard to be mad when he said it like that. We'd bonded because he'd tried to comfort a scared, lonely little girl and I couldn't be angry with him for that. My wrath faded as quickly as it had come.

'Your mum had heard the prophecy only days before. That was why she called me that night.'

'Because a griffin was mentioned in the prophecy,' I said dully.

'Yes, and I was the only one she knew.'

'And in doing so, the prophecy was fulfilled,' I grumped.

He shrugged. 'However it came about, I can't bring myself to regret it. Your mother consulted with her grimoire—' he gave me a small smile '—the one you haven't told me about that lives in your safe, and he gave her a rune to use to suppress the bond.'

'For both of us?' I asked suddenly, my heart hammering.

He flushed. 'No. If the bond had been suppressed for both of us there was a risk that it would be damaged, which could harm us both. *Your* bond to *me* was suppressed.'

Embarrassment heated my cheeks. A familiar bond allows both parties to sense each other, to know what the other is feeling. It is designed so that a witch can protect their familiar and vice versa. It was galling to think that Bastion had known my every flash of anger, of sorrow, of desire. He'd had my emotions singing in his head for more than thirty years. He had them now, in this moment, while I battled with shock and hurt.

He'd known me in a far deeper way this whole time and I'd barely known him at all. Hell, I'd consigned him to death, leaving him to suffer under a black witch's curse. What if he'd died and I'd never known he was my familiar? Guilt surged through me.

Bastion held my hand. 'Don't feel bad. It wasn't your fault. It was your mum's decision and I respected it.'

Anger and bitterness lashed through me again. 'Because it was easier to suppress the bond than be bound to a child,' I accused.

'Whether you knew it or not, I *was* bound to a child,' he snarled back, his own anger rising. 'I've been your familiar for three decades. You never noticed that it was always *me* that saved you, Amber? When vampyrs and necromancers and werewolves threatened you, it was always *me* pulling you out of the fire. Always.'

He shook his head in frustration. 'Sometimes I was on the other side of the world, Bambi, when your fear sent me scrambling for the skies, running to you. For a long time I found it hard to come to terms with – I wasn't used to being at *anyone*'s beck and call, let alone a child's. But being with you these last few weeks, guarding you openly, has been such a relief. Getting to know you properly rather than simply having flashes of feelings that weren't my own... Being with you.' He met my eyes with a passion that sizzled. 'I've felt happier than I have for so long.'

'I don't know what to say.' I blew out a breath. 'I'm sorry it was a burden. Now I don't know which way is up.'

I guarded my emotions, partly because of my father's abandonment and partly because of Mum's illness and my lack of a familiar. I was an intensely private person; knowing that he'd been privy to my emotions the whole time was a bitter pill to swallow.

Melva had remained respectfully silent but now she spoke up. Frankly, I'd forgotten she was there. 'You'll need time to process it, of course, but you haven't spoken of the rest of the prophecy.'

I frowned. 'It's not about me though, is it? It's about the Crone.'

Melva looked sympathetic. 'Amber, the whole prophecy is about you.'

'But the Crone—' I trailed off. Abigay, the Crone, was dead and gone but she would have a replacement.

Melva continued drawing out what I was too stubborn to see. 'The Crone is *you*, child. What I don't know is whether it will be this appointment or the next or the one after that. But one day you will bear the mantle of the Crone and all the power and responsibility that comes with it.'

Wonderful, I thought drily.

Chapter 18

At one stage in my life, being told I was going to be someone as important as the Crone would have filled me with excitement. Think of all the good I could do! But instead all I felt was tired, bone-achingly tired. Abigay was the Crone; she had deserved that title and I hated that she was gone. I wasn't the Crone, I couldn't be because it was Abigay's role... It was fair to say I hadn't come to terms with her death.

Even if I accepted what Melva had said was true, I couldn't see it happening any time soon. The Crone had always been a respected witch, a formidable one, a woman in her sixties with gravitas and a lifetime of experience to pull on. I was in my forties and a lowly Coven Mother. I wasn't even on the Council – not that Abigay had been on it before her appointment, but that was different. Abigay had been one of Edinburgh's movers and shakers years before she became Crone. The only thing I'd been was on trial.

What I *could* take from the prophecy was that it was my destiny to weed out black witches. I'd been on a roll with that lately: first Ria, then Hilary, then Becky. The prophecy said the black witches trembled at the thought of me, which seemed faintly ridiculous. They were afraid of a woman who wore flowing skirts, devoured blueberry muffins and romance books? I wasn't someone to fear. Or I hadn't been.

It was a huge shift in my thinking to realise that I wasn't just an ally to the predators – maybe I was one as well. Maybe they *should* fear me. But they could fear me later, after I'd saved Melva and had some sleep.

'My 4pm will be arriving any minute,' Melva said. 'You have to go.'

I folded my arms. Absolutely no chance. 'No.'

'No?'

'No,' I repeated. 'I'm not leaving you, not until I've made sure you stay alive.'

She crossed the distance between us and hugged me. 'Thank you, Amber.'

'For what?' I asked, but my throat was thick and my eyes were prickling.

'For caring.' She squeezed me. 'You can't save everyone,' she murmured gently.

'I can try.' Even I could hear the desperation in my voice.

'If it makes you feel better.' She sighed then muttered to herself, 'It's not as if my reputation for maintaining client confidentiality is going to matter soon.' She cleared her throat. 'You can wait in my private orb room but you must be quiet.'

'Behind the bookcase?'

She blinked. 'Yes. How did you know?'

'A little imp told me,' I replied facetiously.

She frowned but nodded at the bookcase. 'Just walk through it. It's an illusion.'

I grimaced; I despise walking through anything that appears solid. I had a sudden flashback to Benji heaving me through the walls of Edinburgh and tried to stifle the surge of fear the memory brought. That hadn't been fun.

Bastion's fingers laced through mine, no doubt because he'd felt my trepidation. When all this was over, I was going to undo that suppression rune so that it was a two-way street. I hated that he had access to my thoughts when I had no access to his.

I squeeze his hand. 'Pull me through?' I asked softly.

'Of course. Close your eyes.'

I squinched them shut as he tugged me forward and let my feet follow his lead. I felt the air cool slightly. 'You can open your eyes,' he murmured, his breath against my cheek.

The walls were lined with shelves filled with glowing orbs. I guessed this was where the prophecies lived before they were formally filed with the Hall of Prophecy. Melva had never put mine in an orb; she'd held it inside herself this whole time.

Where the bookcase illusion was, a transparent wall allowing us to look directly into Melva's office. 'Can you hear us?' I called.

'Yes,' Melva confirmed tartly. 'So no heavy petting back there!' She smirked. 'I'm going to call in my 4pm.'

She used the intercom to tell Nell to let in her next client. 'But your 3pm...' Nell argued, sounding confused.

'The appointment has finished,' Melva responded firmly. 'Send in the 4pm and then you can finish for the day. Thank you so much for all your hard work, Nell.'

I grimaced. She was thanking Nell not just for today but for everything she had done. Despite having Bastion and me in her corner, Melva still thought she was going to die. I bet Jinx didn't have to deal with this cynicism when *she* rescued someone.

Chapter 19

Bastion stayed tense and ready behind the illusionary bookcase, poised to leap through if the 4pm ended up being an appointment with death. It was not. It was Mr and Mrs Gilden, who wanted to know if their baby daughter had bred true and was going to be a wizard.

Melva held the babe, looking into her eyes, then intoned some Latin and anointed the six-month-old with oil, at which point the kid started wailing. Melva passed the baby back to her mother and brought out a crystal ball. I noted with approval that it had been safely secured in a cloth bag inside a drawer. No accidental crystal-ball fires here.

Melva looked into it for five long minutes. Even I started wondering about the fate of Gilden Junior as various expressions danced across her face. Finally she slumped back in her seat and covered the ball.

'Well?' Mr Gilden asked eagerly. 'Is she?'

'She's a wizard,' Melva confirmed with a smile.

'Thank God!' Mrs Gilden murmured, cuddling her baby close. 'If she was a Common realmer it would have been so hard to keep magic from her. I would have hated it.'

I was glad to hear that her main concern had been that, rather than building up a wizard dynasty. It wasn't unheard of for children that hadn't bred true to be put up for adoption. At times the Other realm could be cold and hard.

Melva gave some cryptic words of advice to guide the young child and the Gildens left. The baby didn't have a prophecy of her own. *Lucky her*, I thought mutinously.

The Seer busied herself making a cup of chamomile tea while we stayed hidden and silent in the orb room. She drank her tea then ate a bar of chocolate. It riled me: she was drinking her favourite drink and eating her favourite food as if she really thought she was going to die. She had Bastion in her corner. She wasn't going to need a last meal.

Melva pulled out her phone and sent off a few messages, then put it down and waited. Her hands were folded in her lap and she was gazing a little to her left. I swallowed. She knew what was coming.

She wasn't kept waiting long.

A vampyr slid out of the shadows to her left. His eyes were jet black; he was being controlled by a necromancer. 'Bastion!' I shouted but I needn't have bothered – he was already moving.

Vampyrs are insanely fast, though, and he had phased out of the shadows right next to Melva. He had a syringe in his hand; he stabbed it into her neck and pushed down the plunger.

I ran through the illusionary wall, opening my tote as fast as I could. I plunged my hand inside and wrestled out the potion jars. Bastion was already on the vampyr, fury written on his features. His chest heaving, he tore its head clean off its shoulders.

As I looked at Melva, she smiled at me. Her chest rose once and she gave a gasp, then her chest didn't rise again. 'No!' I pleaded. 'No, I'm here to *save* you! Don't die, Melva!' Her glassy eyes ignored my heartfelt pleas.

No doubt it was exhaustion that made the tears pour down my face. I was just so damned tired. I went to touch her neck, to check for a pulse before I let myself give up – even I couldn't heal death – but Bastion gently pushed my hand away.

'Don't touch the body. The last thing we need is another trial because your prints are found on it,' he said grimly. His expression softened. 'She's gone, Bambi.'

'But…'

'She's gone,' he repeated with absolute certainty. 'I can reach out with my magic but I can't coax her. There's no life to coax with.'

Next to him, the vampyr's corpse disappeared into dust. 'We'd better tidy that up,' I said absently. 'Nell will go mad if we leave all that dust.'

Bastion nodded then his arms circled me and he tucked me under his chin. We stayed like that for several minutes. My heart was hurting.

'We need to tidy,' I repeated. There hadn't been a pile of dust when we'd arrived at 8pm.

Bastion gave me one last squeeze before he stepped out of the room. He found a vacuum cleaner somewhere in one of the offices and I watched, still in shock, as he calmly removed all the vampyr dust. Dust to dust, ashes to hoover bag.

While he cleaned, I checked the wards on Melva's room. Sure enough, the vampyr-repelling wards had been cancelled with a neatly inscribed *ezro*. Her offices were a commercial property so without the active ward there had been nothing to stop her killer from phasing in. She'd had a meeting with the vampyrs earlier on that day; no doubt she'd had the wards cancelled for that. She should have met them off site. She should have told me she'd had the anti-vampyr runes cancelled. It was a grave mistake that had led to her death.

But *I* should have checked the runes. I knew an attack was coming, so why didn't I check the damned runes? What was I thinking? I rubbed a hand across my face. I was exhausted. My brain wasn't working at optimum capacity and, because of that, Melva was dead.

Bastion hoovered on, sparing me worried glances now and again. I wanted to wave away his concern because I deserved the guilt that was swamping me. I'd dropped the ball and now Melva was dead.

When the room was pristine – apart from the body at the desk – we went back into the orb room again to await our own arrival and a startled Frogmatch. We talked quietly until eight o'clock rolled around, and then we waited in silence.

Nobody tells you how crushing it is when you can't save someone. I'd experienced it before, of course; even potions and magic can't save everyone. I'd had people die on me before. But Melva ... it was personal. I had been so sure that our jaunt through time would save her.

Her destiny had had other ideas.

Chapter 20

It is incredibly disconcerting to watch yourself walk and talk with other people. After past-Amber and past-Bastion finally left the office, there was a narrow window of escape while the CSI guys popped back to their van. If we didn't move then, we'd be stuck for hours and hours.

Bastion moved silently and I tried to emulate him, wincing at every noise I made. He swore under his breath as he heard someone approaching and pulled us hastily into some sort of utilities cupboard. I was precariously balanced next to a mop bucket and I recognised the hoover we'd used to suck up the vampyr.

He closed the door behind us and we tensed, waiting to see if we'd been spotted. The space was limited and I was pressed up against him. There were worse places to be. 'This is nice,' I said facetiously. 'You definitely do dates better than Emory.'

He stilled. 'After everything, do you still want to go on a date with me?'

That was a loaded question and I took a moment to really think about it, to think about all we'd been through together and what he'd come to mean to me.

I seized all of my courage and faced him. Cracks of light were beaming into the cupboard from the hallway and I could see the hard lines of his face, the scar through his lip, the sprinkle of grey in his hair. He was gloriously, ridiculously handsome, and it bowled me over that he had any interest in me.

'Yes,' I replied. 'I still want to go on a date with you. If you'll have me.'

'For a long time you were just the kid I was bonded to,' he admitted. 'Then you were the witch I was bonded to. Now you're Amber.' Emotion I couldn't – wouldn't – name swelled in his voice. 'My Bambi. Yes. Please.'

I had never heard him say that word, not once, and it was its own brand of magic. Hearing him say please made my knees go weak. I wanted to hear it more. Something hot curled in my belly and I licked my lips.

His lips curved in response. 'Not here,' he whispered. 'We're not having our first kiss in a supplies closet.' His voice was low and husky; he wanted it as much as I did. For a moment I was tempted to press the point, but he went on, 'Besides, I want this rune off when we share our first kiss. I want you to feel me, Amber, like I feel you.'

The man had more patience than a saint. 'Then let's get out of here,' I growled, since my own patience had long since dissipated.

The CSI guy had disappeared again so Bastion cautiously opened the cupboard door, took my hand and led me through a small staff kitchen. He transformed his right hand into a claw and used it, somewhat clumsily, to open the back door. 'No fingerprints,' he explained.

'Animals have fingerprints too, you know. Koalas have unique prints just like us. And orangutans.'

'How do you know that?'

My brain holds all sorts of useless information. 'How do you not?' I shot back, making him grin.

'I won't be leaving any fingerprints that are in the Connection or police system.'

Once we were outside, we paused in the car park behind the office. We had no transport. I didn't want to call the Coven and ask for the van while two of me were running around. I guessed we could always grab a taxi or walk to a bus stop.

Bastion shimmered and then he stood on four legs. 'Climb on,' he instructed.

I blinked. I guess that solved our transport issue. 'But we haven't even had our date yet,' I protested.

He snorted, wings ruffling, and I climbed on. 'Hold tight.'

I didn't have his harness to secure me but we wouldn't be flying far. Bastion waited until I'd grasped the tufts of hair at the apex of his back then launched himself forward, gaining speed before his wings snapped out and started to lift us.

In a minute we were high in the sky, above the grey wet clouds we'd pushed through. It was weird: I knew that clouds are made of water but they looked so fluffy and white that I didn't expect rain to hit my skin as we'd ploughed through one of them. A fine mist clung to my face and clothes. Then we broke through the bank of grey and the sun beamed at us. Above every grey day, a glorious one waited.

We didn't fly for long before Bastion dived back down. I squeezed his body tightly with my legs and silenced the scream that wanted to tear out of my throat. Exhilaration rushed through me as we ploughed back through the soggy clouds. Finally he landed lightly and expertly on top of the Coven roof.

I slid off his back and he shifted to human. I couldn't help but beam at him. 'That was awesome.'

'You prefer it without the harness?'

'I don't know. I think last time the circumstances weren't great, so I wasn't exactly focused on the ride.'

A smirk tugged at his lips. 'If you liked that ride, just you wait.'

I huffed. 'You're all talk. My lips remain unkissed. I'm beginning to think you don't even like me.'

In a second he was on me, his body pressed against mine. He shifted his hips and suddenly I could feel something hot, hard and huge against my hip. 'Oh,' I said, eyes wide.

'Oh,' he agreed. 'Having you ride me is – stimulating. Don't think me cold or unaffected, Amber. I want you so much it is distracting me, but we can't afford distractions, not now.' He stepped back. 'Let's go and get this bloody rune off me.'

He grabbed my hand and tugged me into the Coven's tower. He was a man on a mission.

Chapter 21

Luckily we didn't encounter a soul on our way in. Bastion entered the code to my apartment, unlocked the door and the scent of home welcomed me. Something in me eased.

'Have you got some healing potions handy?' Bastion asked.

'Of course.'

'Good. I'll do it in the bathroom. Bring the potions.'

Do what in the bathroom? I hastily pulled out my strongest healing potion from the fridge, grabbed some brushes and followed him. He was moving the bathroom mat to one side. Without a hint of self-consciousness, he kicked off his boots and socks, unbuckled his trousers and pulled them off. He still wore tight black boxers and I tried hard not to stare. He folded his clothes neatly and stepped into the bath.

His eyes flashed gold and his right hand shifted into his talons. With a glance at me, he rolled up the bottom edge of his boxers to expose the rune on his inner thigh and I suddenly realised what he was going to do. Before I could object, he used his talon to slice off the flesh of his inner thigh. The runed flesh fell to the bottom of the bathroom and blood poured from the wound.

'Bastion! I could have just painted an *ezro!*' I complained.

Before I could approach him with my potions, he shifted into griffin form to start the healing process. I gaped a little at the sight of a huge griffin squashed into my bathtub. 'Why did you have me bring healing potions?' I asked in exasperation.

'Just giving you something to do,' he explained cheekily.

I was amused – but then I realised it wasn't *my* humour I was experiencing but *his*. My eyes widened as I stared at him. 'I can feel you!' I gasped.

'I should hope so. I'd be disappointed if I'd just sliced off a pound of flesh for no reason at all.'

Bastion shifted back to his human form and stood in my shower wearing his black T-shirt and boxers. I let my eyes rove over the muscles of his thighs; not a mark remained of the gruesome wound that had been there moments before.

No wonder griffins were such fierce warriors; with healing like that they hardly needed to fear any wounds, bar a killing blow.

'Amber, if you don't stop staring at me like that, I'm not going to be held responsible for my actions.'

I felt the stirrings of arousal: his, not mine. 'We have time,' I murmured. 'Come and be irresponsible with me.'

'Temptress.' Bastion reached down, grasped the bottom of his T-shirt and peeled it over his head. He stared at me, his gaze hot as he saw me admiring the hard lines of his chest. 'Yes,' he agreed. 'Let's be irresponsible – but after we've cleaned up here.'

He turned on the water on and washed away the blood. I felt the skin under my collar grow hot as I watched him scrub the bath. Honestly, something was wrong with me: there shouldn't have been anything remotely sexy about Bastion cleaning my bath.

I grabbed the superfluous jars of healing potion, took them into the kitchen area and put them back into the fridge. I held the fridge door open for a few moments – I needed to cool down.

Bastion padded out after me, still in his boxers and nothing more. I appreciated his lack of clothes; the man was model-fit. I hoped I wasn't visibly drooling as I watched his corded muscles flex and roll when he moved.

'Wine?' he asked as he sauntered into my kitchen.

'Champagne,' I countered.

'What are we celebrating?'

I thought of Melva. 'That we're alive.'

He nodded gravely. 'Yes.'

Bastion pulled a bottle out of the fridge, opened it expertly and poured two flutes of champagne. He brought them over, handed me one then slid onto the sofa and took a sip from his glass. I felt his enjoyment as the cool bubbly liquid slid down his throat. I gulped, hard.

'I can feel that you enjoyed that,' I whispered, eyes wide. Every time he'd feel pleasure, I'd feel it too. I'd know exactly what he liked and he would know the same about me. Oh boy.

His eyes smouldered. 'I know.'

I swallowed hard and knew that he wasn't feeling trepidation from me as he might once have done. Instead he could sense my excitement, my desire.

I took a sip of my champagne and sat next to him. I was breathing a little more heavily, my heart beating a little faster. I was suddenly aware that I was wearing entirely too many clothes compared to Bastion.

He was making himself as non-threatening as he could. He'd removed his weapons and his clothes, and he was waiting patiently, letting me make the first move if I wanted to. He was taking 'no pressure' to a whole new level.

What I wanted, though, was for him to kiss me. I wanted him to kiss me more than I could recall wanting anything else ever. I looked at him and hoped that I was communicating that to him somehow. It had been twenty long years since I'd last been touched. I wanted it to happen but I lacked the confidence to seize the moment. I needed him to make the first move.

I met his eyes. 'Please,' I begged softly.

Bastion's eyes darkened. He took the champagne flute from me and set it down on the table then studied me, as he was wont to do. My chest was rising and falling a little too fast. He missed nothing. His hands slipped under me and he effortlessly lifted me so that I was straddling his lap.

I could feel his desire, not just in the hard warmth nuzzling against me, but in a roar inside my own body. My own desire was shouting just as loudly; it was taking every bit of self-restraint within me not to chuck myself at him like a groupie at a concert. But I wanted this to be good, to be right. We only get one first kiss; we'd delayed it for so long that it had to be perfect – a standard I had no doubt Bastion could attain.

His eyes were dark brown, flecked with hints of his shifted golden eyes. Those eyes that missed nothing flicked down to my lips and I felt the steady thrum of his emotions through our bond. There was more than desire there; I sensed his affection, his loyalty, and an underlying current of something more, something I was too scared to label.

Achingly slowly, giving me plenty of time to pull away, Bastion lowered his lips, softly to mine. My eyes closed as I pressed my lips to his in answer. The kiss deepened as our tongues tangled and a delicious shudder ran through me. I moaned aloud. It felt like his tongue had a direct link to the heat between my legs.

As the kiss continued, something within us ignited. A mutual hunger burned between us, our connection amplifying every sensation, sending us into a maelstrom of heat and fire.

I felt his quandary moments before he forced himself to pull away. 'We should go slow,' he managed.

I could feel his desire, voracious and hot like mine but tempered with the need to be respectful, to take care of me, to do this right. 'Fuck slow,' I responded firmly, pulling him back down to my wanton lips. I had never been so sure of anything in my life. I kissed him with all the passion and need that was coiled within me.

His chest vibrated as he laughed silently. 'I can do that,' he promised teasingly.

'Thank the Goddess!'

'Are you sure, Amber?' he asked, studying me.

'Yes.'

'You can tell me to stop at any time and I will. Straight away.'

'I know.' I paused. 'I won't though. I'm done waiting. If we went any slower, we'd turn into a glacier. Kiss me,' I demanded.

'Yes ma'am.' His lips found mine again. This time, I wasn't letting him pull away.

Chapter 22

I was pulled from sleep by the irritatingly shrill beep of my phone alarm. Without opening my eyes, I picked up the phone and launched it through the open doorway and out of the room. Bastion and I had barely slept all night, and a delicious ache was pervading any number of muscles that I hadn't used in a very, very long time.

Amusement flared in my chest, in the part of me that I thought of as Bastion's. He found me chucking away my phone funny. He would have found it even funnier if he'd known I was aiming for the wall.

I felt more solid today, and I realised that now there was only one of me running around the world. The jaunt through time had been necessary, but the prickling of my skin that told of two of me existing hadn't been comfortable. I was relieved the sensation had vanished. Then

I wondered where Frogmatch was; I hoped he was safely ensconced with Oscar.

'Morning, Bambi.' Bastion pressed a kiss to my neck in that spot that he'd found I liked, making me arch my back in a pool of desire. 'You're insatiable,' he murmured as his hands stroked the length of my body.

'Are you complaining?'

'Not for a single second,' he promised solemnly. 'But you're sore.'

'A little,' I admitted.

His hands paused. 'Let's get you some healing salve.'

'Only if you promise to be the one that applies it,' I suggested archly.

He grinned. 'You read my mind.'

We showered together, hot water sluicing us. The first time we'd showered and tried to get clean, we'd ended up getting very, very dirty instead. This time we actually managed to use the shower for its true purpose.

When we stepped out, I dried, runed myself and got dressed. I sat in front of the mirror and contemplated my affirmations. For once, I didn't have to say them. I had a familiar and it wouldn't be true to affirm that I didn't need anyone, not any more. I needed Bastion, and I needed

Oscar and Benji and Jinx and Lucy. Heck, maybe even Frogmatch would make the list.

I looked at my reflection and crafted a new affirmation. 'I am a strong, successful witch. With my friends and family beside me, I am unstoppable. I *will* change this world for the better.' I smiled. Go big or go home. I was aiming for the moon; here's hoping I'd land in the stars.

I sashayed out of my bedroom into the living room and took a breathless moment to admire the man manoeuvring around my kitchen like a pro. Like he'd manoeuvred around me.

'What's the plan for the day?' Bastion asked, his tone businesslike as he passed me a glass of fresh orange juice and a bowl of overnight oats.

The oats gave me pause. When exactly had Oscar sneaked them into my fridge? My cheeks warmed and Bastion grinned as he felt my embarrassment. 'Oscar knows about the birds and the bees.'

'Yes, but he doesn't need to know that *I* know about them,' I muttered.

'You're forty-two. He knows.'

I humphed and dived into my raspberry-flavoured oats. I was far hungrier than usual. I must have used a lot more energy than usual and my body wanted to refuel. I drained my orange juice and thought about my plans for the day.

Much as I wanted to lounge around naked in my flat with Bastion – and I really did want to do that – I had too much to do to spend time indulging myself. 'I need to finish the final-defence potion. The base will only be fresh enough for another day or two, max. That's top of the list. If you want, you can summon Shirdal to come and get his replacement vial.' I owed him that and much more for saving Bastion.

'And after that?'

'After that is finding the necromancer that killed Melva.'

'Do you have a plan for accomplishing that?' Bastion asked curiously.

I grimaced. 'Yeah. We're going to speak to Voltaire. Krieg said he'd reach out to him for us, but so far we haven't heard anything. Can you set up a meet?'

He nodded. 'Leave it with me. I'll line something up while you finish the potion.'

'Thank you. I knew I could rely on you.'

He picked up our dirty bowls and pressed a light kiss to my forehead. 'Always,' he murmured as he walked away.

I watched him clean our dirty dishes, his calloused hands carefully wiping away the remnants of the oats with a sudsy cloth. 'Lucky dishes,' I muttered. A surge of amusement and shaking shoulders told me that Bastion had heard my comment. Stupid supernatural hearing.

I bit my lip as desire swelled. 'I think I have a cleaning kink,' I admitted. 'Is that a thing?'

'Kinks come in all shapes and sizes. You decide what's yours.' He shot me a look with his bedroom eyes. 'I'm perfectly happy to clean dishes if it gets you fired up.'

'Like a bonfire,' I admitted.

'I'm going to clean the whole flat while you make potions,' he promised.

I groaned. With considerable effort, I tore my eyes away from him and tried to bring my errant thoughts back to my day. I reluctantly went through my office to my lab, leaving Bastion to clean and sort out an appointment with Voltaire. I exhaled in relief when I saw the base of the potion was still in stasis. It would be fine.

Before I started work, I pulled out my phone and texted Oscar. *Did you get back okay from Liverpool?* No need to be more specific than that.

No problem, came the instant reply. *I'm Coven side. Frogmatch is with me. Let me know if you need me.*

I'll need a trip to Rosie's soon, I admitted. I hated using the portal and being stuck in the Common realm, but I'd used a huge amount of magic recently and I'd be using more to finish the final-defence potion. I'd already drunk my vial of ORAL potion, so I'd need a proper recharge.

Just let me know when.

Relieved that Oscar and Frogmatch were safe in the tower – though I'd already been pretty sure of that from the orange juice and oats in my fridge – I turned my mind to potion making. I slipped out of my heavy skirt, leaving me in my leggings, before I removed the cauldron lid and broke the stasis spell.

I lit a fire under the pewter cauldron to start warming its contents then pulled a ladder over to my ingredient store. I climbed up, selected half-a-dozen ingredients including the incredibly rare kiteen leaves, and carried them to my immaculate workstation. Paranoia made me clean the surface again before I started work; I couldn't risk this potion being contaminated.

I slipped the thermometer into its wooden frame and swung it so that the end dipped into the potion's surface. It was still far too cool for me to add anything, so I busied myself with the rest of the preparations. My hands were steady as I lifted the purple kiteen leaf out of its safe storage.

I set it down on the work surface and started the painfully slow process of cutting away the leaf, leaving nothing but its broad veins. I tried to stay relaxed: one wrong slice would break the veins and the potion would be ruined.

With this potion I could save Bastion's life, and Shirdal's too. And other griffins, ones I hadn't met, who were as worthy of the life-saving potion as the two griffins who'd wormed their way into my affections.

It was hard to believe how stubborn I had once been, how blind to Bastion's kindness. I had ignored everything he'd done, even when he'd saved my life time and time again. It was painful to contemplate how wrong I'd been, not just because I despised being wrong, but because I'd wronged Bastion. And I still hadn't found either the time or the words to apologise to the man who had taken residence in my heart.

The sharp blade nearly slipped and I snarled inwardly; now was not the time to go wool-gathering. *Focus, Amber DeLea.*

It took a very long half hour to cut away the leaf's exoskeleton, and the whole time my heart was thundering. One mistake would render the ingredient useless and the potion would be over before it had even begun. But I was no blushing acolyte, and after forty minutes of careful work the network of veins was exposed.

Whoever had worked out that the veins of the leaf were powerful whilst the flesh of the leaf nullified them was a veritable genius. Whoever they were, their name was lost to history – but I would not suffer the same fate. I had created the ORAL potion; I was the first witch to make the final-defence potion in nearly a decade, and I was the first witch in living memory to have a magical creature familiar.

My name might be remembered but so would Bastion's. I'd make sure of it.

Chapter 23

I decanted the last of the potion into the special round vials that were as much a signature of the final-defence potion as the blackish sludgy liquid inside them. Each vial was the precise dose for a griffin, and one dose would save them from a potentially fatal injury.

The dark liquid did not have the same properties if it was imbibed by any other species; it helped and healed, certainly, but it couldn't bring them back from the brink of death. There was something in the griffins that was unique to them, their innate connection to death, perhaps. The final-defence potion enhanced that link and allowed them another chance to dodge death.

I had made as much potion as the leaf would allow, measuring each ingredient with razor-sharp precision. Eighteen little vials sat before me and I pocketed one of them. Bastion was irritatingly honourable and I had no doubt that he would only take one vial. He was guarding my life, and we were about to go head-to-head with another black witch. One vial wasn't enough. Thinking about it, two vials weren't enough. I put another vial in my desk drawer. Just to be safe.

I placed the remaining sixteen vials in a special potion pouch made of selkie skin, a rare commodity these days, that was warded with runes to keep the contents unbroken. Such runes painted onto leather had little effect, but selkie skin was another matter. Runes are fickle things.

I felt my wards buzz with a distinctly griffinish air. I knew the feel of that particular griffin. I touched the walls and, with a trickle of my magic, allowed Shirdal into my home.

I cleaned up the laboratory and, when everything shone, I pulled on my skirt. Dressed appropriately, I went back into my office and out to the living room. My balcony door was open and Fehu was resting contentedly on Bastion's shoulder.

Shirdal was sitting opposite them, sprawled with one leg across the chair's arm. His clothing was rumpled, his hair unbrushed; if the man would only make a little effort, he'd be quite charming. I had no doubt that *he* wouldn't be cleaning up anytime soon.

Shirdal had a way about him, a relaxed air that eased tensions. He couldn't possibly be a deadly griffin; he was a drunk and a bum. He let everyone around him underestimate him and then, when the going got tough, so did he. It was quite the transformation that I'd seen on a few occasions, enough to know not to trust the image he projected.

'Shirdal,' I greeted him.

'Sweetheart! It's good to see you.'

I smiled. I didn't mind him using that moniker. I held the pouch up for him, gratified to see his eyes widen as he realised what it was. I drew it to my heart and held it there for five seconds with my eyes closed, imbuing it with as much of my protective magic as I dared.

When I opened my eyes, Shirdal was standing up, sharp, solemn and still. By the Goddess, this was the real Shirdal, not the other one. There was no sign of the swaying drunkard; he had drawn himself up to his full height and he looked regal.

The room pulsed with his power and my scalp prickled with the strength of his aura. How could anyone doubt him, doubt his moral fibre? It literally shone from him, his greatness exposed for the world to see. And then I blinked and it was gone.

My heart was pounding and I realised that invoking the Goddess, even in my thoughts, had brought her awareness to me. For whatever reason, she had chosen to show me Shirdal's true self. It was a timely reminder that the person we present to the world is rarely the whole of us. Instead, it is a shadow of ourselves, the facet of ourselves that we *choose* to present. Our true light is reserved for ourselves and our loved ones.

I stepped forward to the leader of the griffins with ceremonial slowness. When I was within a foot of him, I curtsied deeply to show the respect that was now humming in my heart. 'Shirdal, *rahbar-e mo'azzam*. Leader of the griffins, I gift to you sixteen vials of final-defence and the pouch in which they reside.'

I hoped I'd pronounced his title correctly. Bastion had taught me a few phrases in the dead of the night, but languages had never been my strong point.

'Gift?' His tone was flabbergasted.

'Gift,' I confirmed.

Shirdal touched his hand to his heart, stepped back and bowed low. 'Amber DeLea, *aziz e-delam*.' His voice cracked with emotion. 'I am truly honoured by your gift.' He rose to his full height, reverently took the bag from me and cradled it against his heart. 'I will see these are shared among my people. This gift will not be forgotten.'

He bowed again then strode to Bastion and held out the pouch to him. Bastion reached in, took one potion and bowed to Shirdal. 'These are a gift from your *zan*. You may take another,' Shirdal said solemnly.

As expected, Bastion shook his head. 'No, *rahbar*. They will all find a worthy home. I have only need of one.'

Three, I thought smugly. He didn't know it, but he had three: the one he'd taken and the two I'd snagged for him.

Shirdal didn't argue. He simply nodded, pocketed one of the vials and shifted into griffin form. He took two steps onto my balcony and jumped off it. His wings snapped out and he flew away effortlessly; such was his haste to get the life-saving vials to his people that he didn't even say farewell. Pride stirred in my heart. I'd done a good thing.

Bastion looked at me. 'Thank you, Amber.' His voice vibrated with sincerity. 'That you would do this means a great deal to me. You will save lives, the lives of my brothers and sisters in arms. I cannot thank you enough for this gift.'

I shifted uncomfortably. I was only doing what was right; surely anyone would do the same. 'It's just a potion. I'm a potion mistress. It's no problem,' I said lightly.

His eyes were still fervent, but he sensed how uncomfortable I was with his gratitude so he moved on. 'We're going to work on that,' he murmured.

'Work on what?'

'Accepting compliments and gratitude. One day you'll know I mean it when I say you're beautiful.'

Heat flushed my cheeks as it did every time he admired me. 'You're delusional but that's okay. I like you that way.'

He grinned. 'Good. Now...' His eyes narrowed. 'How many of the vials did you keep for me?'

He surprised a laugh out of me; he really did know me. 'Two others,' I admitted.

He closed the distance between us. 'Thank you, Bambi.' He leaned down and kissed me, long and slow, until my mind went blank. If that was the way he thanked me, I'd give him as many potions as he wanted.

When he pulled away, his eyes were warm and affectionate. 'You surprised Shirdal,' he noted.

'Did I?' I breathed, still revelling in the taste of his lips.

'Yes. He thought you were going to give him mates' rates, not the whole lot for free.' He paused. 'Will you be in trouble with the Coven Council? You just gave away more than fifteen million pounds in Coven revenue.'

I sniffed. 'It's not the Coven's revenue, it's *mine*. The black kiteen leaf was gifted to *me* by Peter, not to the Coven. Besides, when you lay dying, I begged Shirdal to save you, to give you his last defence. In return, I promised I would brew him a cauldron of final-defence.'

'Even so, he expected you to charge for it.'

I shook my head. 'It didn't feel right.'

Bastion tipped my chin up, 'For all you make the right mercenary noises, you're nothing but a soft-hearted kitten.'

'Says you, Mr Marshmallow.'

He grinned. 'I'm only soft for you, Amber.'

I raised an eyebrow. 'Oh?' I purred. 'I rather thought I had the opposite effect on you.'

His eyes darkened. 'Let me show you what effect you have on me.'

'Sure. Go ahead. I've often heard that communication is important in a healthy relationship.'

'It is,' he agreed. 'I'm going to communicate at length.'

'Promises, promises.' A laugh bubbled out of me.

He grabbed my hand and tugged me to the bedroom. I didn't resist in the slightest.

Chapter 24

'I have to come clean about something,' Bastion said, clearing his throat nervously.

'What?' I asked.

'You know that the griffin numbers are very low?'

'Yes?'

'They're not as low as people think.'

'What?' I pushed myself up on one elbow. 'What do you mean?'

'People are ... threatened by us. We're fairly scary. But not all griffins want to be assassins when they grow up.'

I blinked. Not every witch made potions; some did runes, others did crystal-ball work, others became healers, and a few of us didn't have a magical job at all. 'No, of course not. That makes sense.'

'Those of us that choose the warrior's path are openly griffins. But those of us that don't...' He trailed off.

'Hide it?' I offered. I helped to administer an underground circus for Other realm runaways so I knew all about the need to hide sometimes.

'Yes,' he confirmed.

'What do they pretend to be? Wizards?' I guessed.

'No. The IR is next to impossible to fake. That's why we've knelt to the Prime Elite. Emory hides us as brethren.'

The Prime Elite title made Emory more than just the Prime, the king of the dragons; the 'Elite' meant he was king of other creatures as well, including the griffins. Emory seemed to be a fair ruler but it had always perplexed me why the deadly griffins would want – or need – his protection. Now it made sense.

Brethren are offspring of dragons that haven't bred true. They are more than human but less than dragons. They live longer and they have an extra helping of toughness that helps them survive the Other realm. Almost before they can walk, they have weapons' training.

Hiding griffins as brethren was genius. The brethren are innumerable and they have their own deadly reputation; if a brethren killed someone, no one would think it odd.

'But how do they cope with their deathly urges?' I asked, frowning. 'The brethren don't kill *that* often, except to protect their families and dragons.'

Bastion levelled a serious look at me. 'A lot of the hidden griffins become vets.'

Huh. 'Putting an animal down... Is that enough to expunge the urge?'

'Yes. So much so that there's a rota. If all of the griffin vets in a certain place have curtailed the urge, they call in others. After Charlize was kidnapped, I called one of the vets and got her in.'

I closed my eyes. I had assumed he'd rung Shirdal to find out a target for assassination; instead, she'd been putting a poor animal out of its misery. When would I stop making assumptions?

Bastion cleared his throat. 'But though the low numbers are exaggerated, our fertility issues are real. Griffins struggle to procreate. Although I have Charlize, there's really no guarantee that I can have any more children.'

I wondered why he had started this conversation. I smiled. 'Bastion, I don't want children. I never have. I didn't enjoy my own childhood, and I've never wanted motherhood – I don't have the patience for it. Anyway, that ship has pretty much sailed. I'm forty-two and my ovaries are packing up for a tropical holiday. They're done, and I'm okay with that. Some women are born to be mothers but I'm not one of them. Is that okay with you?'

'You definitely don't want children of your own?' he probed.

'Definitely not.'

'Thank God,' he murmured, kissing my shoulder. 'Because I would try again if that's what you wanted but—'

'Nope,' I interrupted firmly. 'If I ever get maternal, I'll borrow Charlize. How old is she, by the way?'

'She's twenty-three.'

'And her mother?' I asked cautiously.

Bastion looked emotionless. 'She's dead.'

'I'm sorry.' I touched his arm lightly.

'Don't be, she was a bitch.' He shrugged. 'The griffins have a compulsory breeding programme. I was matched with Dakota, but although we were genetically compatible we didn't get on. She died when Charlize was about six months old. She went on a mission and never came back.'

'That must have been tough.'

He hesitated. 'I was glad,' he admitted unhappily. 'I know that makes me a bad person, but I got to raise Charlize without Dakota's venom. My daughter is a good kid. She's made some questionable choices in the past as she's tried to prove herself, but I think she's moving out of that now.' Pride coloured his tone.

'She's been amazing with my mum.'

He smiled. 'Like me, she likes protecting others.'

I shook my head wonderingly. 'How did I ever get you so wrong?'

'You were supposed to,' he pointed out.

'True. We can't have everyone learning that Bastion is a good guy.'

His tone was serious. 'I'm not a good man, not really. I've killed plenty of people, more than I can count. But now that I'm watching over you, you never need fear anything or anyone.'

His fierce protectiveness washed over me with a strength that took my breath away. He would kill to protect me; he would die to protect me. I prayed that my enemies wised up, and he had to do neither.

Chapter 25

Voltaire studied me over a black coffee. His hair was as dark as his drink and his skin was as pale as the discarded milk. He was glaring at me openly, but there was nothing unusual in that.

We'd run into each other a time or two. Voltaire headed a team of the Red Guard, the vampyr elite who were responsible for killing necromancers. Necromancers can possess and control vampyrs like puppets, and understandably vampyrs don't much like that. The last time we'd tangled, the necromancer had ended up dead but not at Voltaire's hand. He'd been a bit pissed off about that.

Frogmatch had insisted on coming to the meeting but agreed to stay out of sight. A vampyr was going around collecting imp tails and, while I doubted it was Voltaire doing the harvesting, I was not going to risk Frogmatch. He was nestled in the folds of my voluminous skirt, hidden from view but close enough for me to feel his warmth through my clothes.

'Speak, witch,' Voltaire ordered.

I narrowed my eyes and deliberately took a slow sip of my cappuccino. Since he was being rude, I would be too.

Instead of asking his permission to rune, which would have been polite, I set the cup back down on the saucer and pulled out a paintbrush and a protection potion from my new tote bag. I painted runes on our wooden table: *ansuz* for communication, *nauthiz* for restriction and *algiz* for protection. That meant anything said at the table couldn't be overheard. I pulled my magic forward and let the runes light up. Their glow told Rosie's Other onlookers that we were discussing things of import, but that couldn't be helped.

I trusted Maxwell, the owner of Rosie's café, but his allegiance was to Roscoe and the Pit, not to me or the Coven Council. He had to do what was right for his people, the fire elementals, and I had to do what was right for mine.

'Touch the table while you speak and none bar us three will hear what is said.' Under the table, Frogmatch emerged from my skirt and leaned up to touch the underside of the table. Four of us, I corrected mentally.

Bastion leaned forward and placed one forearm casually on the table and Voltaire matched his movement. I simply laid my hand on it.

I studied Voltaire before I spoke. He was dressed in black jeans and a black polo shirt, casual-vampyr mode. I'd once seen him in full Red-Guard Regalia and it wasn't an experience I was keen to repeat.

'You got my message from Krieg?' I started finally. The High King of the ogres had promised he would contact Voltaire to help me with my black-witch problem. Voltaire nodded tightly. 'But that wasn't enough to get in touch?' I asked, exasperated.

'You didn't have information,' he growled. 'You wanted help. I don't help witches, I kill them.' He jerked his head towards Bastion. 'I'm only here out of respect for Bastion.' He folded his arms and leaned back then, grimacing, he unfolded his arms and placed one of them back on the table again. Heh.

'I do have information,' I said. 'But I'm only sharing it if you share your information too.' I felt a tug on my shoes and had to resist the urge to look under the table to see what the heck Frogmatch was doing.

'Tell me your information and we'll see,' Voltaire said flatly.

'No, that isn't how this works. We're an equal partnership or we're nothing. Decide,' I ordered abruptly. I sat back but kept my hand lightly on the surface of the wood.

Voltaire was visibly wrestling with himself. With a final glance at Bastion's stony visage, he nodded. 'Fine.'

'Fine, what? Which is it, vampyr?' I asked coolly, drawing the moment out. I couldn't afford to have any mistakes or misunderstandings.

'Partnership.'

I knew a little of vampyr customs; though it was disdainful in the extreme, the only way to bind him properly to his word was with an oath.

'I will share with Voltaire of the Red Guard any and all information I have pertaining to any currently practising black witches or necromancers. I will answer any relevant questions put to me by him with honesty, and I will not seek to omit relevant details. As I will it, so mote it be.' I glowed for a moment as the oath took hold.

With a reluctant twist of his mouth, Voltaire's teeth elongated. He bit into his wrist and blood welled. 'My oath that I will share with Amber DeLea any and all relevant information I have pertaining to any currently practising black witches or necromancers in the United Kingdom. I will answer any relevant questions put to me by her with honesty, and I will not seek to omit relevant details.' He lifted his wrist to his mouth and lapped at it, sealing the wound with his healing spit and not wasting a single drop of his own precious blood.

'Witnessed,' Bastion said gruffly.

Voltaire and I had aligning goals, but I'd heard often enough that he was a vampyr who cared about results and wasn't especially bothered if he made mistakes. He'd killed witches all over Europe. Some may even have been practising black magic. As I stared into his slate-grey eyes, I couldn't help but feel I'd just made a deal with the devil.

Chapter 26

I told Voltaire about the black Coven. I told him about Becky and Hilary, though I didn't tell him about Ria as she wasn't currently a practising black witch. If he knew she ever had been, he would watch her like a hawk and one day she wouldn't come home again. As such, I'd phrased my oath very carefully.

Finally, I told him about my father – as much as I knew, anyway. After all, I didn't care if *he* didn't make it home one day.

'Have you checked your birth certificate?' Voltaire asked tightly.

'The section on her father has been expunged,' Bastion confirmed.

I blinked in surprise. I hadn't known that Bastion had done some digging of his own. Why hadn't that occurred to me? I was running on empty, I guess. 'His name was Shaun. That's all I know,' I said.

'Appearance?'

'He had blond hair and green eyes like mine. Apart from that, it's hazy.'

'Photos?'

I shook my head. 'My mum burned them all when he left us.' I hesitated, but in the spirit of sharing... 'Mum had my mind cleared when he left. That's why I don't remember more.'

'You could get the clearing broken,' Voltaire pointed out.

'No,' Bastion said instantly. 'It would be agonising. It's been in position for too long.'

I touched Bastion's arm lightly. 'It's an option,' I said to Voltaire. 'One I'm exploring. What have you got?'

Voltaire pursed his lips before he began. 'We have long suspected the black Coven's existence. In the last decade or so, we have seen more evidence of collusion amongst black witches. They are organised, they've been working towards a goal.'

'What goal?'

He grimaced. 'If we knew that, it would be a lot easier. Power, certainly.'

'We know *someone* was posing as Felix Holloway on the Coven Council,' Bastion pointed out.

'Indeed. And they orchestrated the Crone's death.' My voice was as emotionless as I could make it.

Voltaire cleared his throat. 'Abigay Morgan was a woman of indomitable strength and presence. I was … saddened to hear of her passing.'

That made me blink. I wasn't sure Voltaire even knew what sadness was. Did the vampyr have a heart somewhere? Surely not. 'Thank you,' I said, acknowledging the effort he was making for us to work together smoothly.

He nodded once. 'Have you heard of the "soul auction"?'

Bastion nodded as I reluctantly shook my head. I despised admitting ignorance but now wasn't the time for pride.

'It is a secret auction of dark artefacts. It is held as and when the artefacts are found. The rumour is that such an auction will be held soon and that a large harkan crystal is on offer.'

My stomach lurched. Now the harkan crystal, I had heard of. Supposedly it was made by collecting one drop of blood at a time from a murder victim then crystallising the drops through magic. The bigger the crystal, the more deaths were required to make it and the greater the power it held. It could be added to over time because more deaths increased its power. Rumour had it that the owner of a harkan crystal never needed recharge in the Common realm.

'Have you been watching the portals to the Common realm?' I asked. 'Is there a witch that doesn't use them?'

Voltaire gave me a distinctly unfriendly look. 'Your ORAL potion has muddied the waters. There are a number of witches that have not attended for some time. Including you.'

I glared at the inference. 'I'm going through the portal after this discussion.'

'No doubt you would claim that.'

'Because it is true!' I rubbed my forehead. 'Enough. When will this so-called "soul auction" take place?'

'It is not simply a matter of finding out when it is occurring,' Voltaire grumbled. 'To gain entrance, you must recently have taken a life.'

I thought of my half-sister, Becky, and the unknown fire elemental before that. 'How recently?'

'Within a few months.'

'That won't be a problem,' I said. Bastion had ripped off a bunch of vampyric heads so he'd be fine to gain entrance too, though I thought it diplomatic not to explain that to Voltaire. 'You find out when and where the auction is and Bastion and I will attend as purchasers.'

Voltaire looked at Bastion. 'He is well known and it is common knowledge that he guards you. If he attends, your identity will be known instantly.'

My flat look told him he was being patronising. 'We will be disguised, obviously.'

'Common sense is not so common.' His mouth tightened but he didn't argue. 'On your heads be it.'

I blinked. 'Did you just quote actual Voltaire at me?'

For the first time that I could recall, I saw a glimmer of humour in the depths of his eyes. 'Are you so sure I'm not the actual Voltaire?'

I opened my mouth then closed it again. He didn't *look* like a seventeenth-century philosopher, but vampyrs could age themselves as they wished. I slid a glance to Bastion who grinned and shook his head. 'He's shitting you.'

'Am I?' Voltaire asked, amused. 'I will send word. When you are summoned, do not hesitate or the opportunity will be lost forever.' He spun on his heels and stalked out.

Someone knew how to make a dramatic exit.

Chapter 27

It turned out that Frogmatch's tugging on my shoes during my meeting with Voltaire had been him making art with my boots. He had apparently lost all interest in our chatter and focused instead on my shoelaces. Resting in Rosie's main apartment, I watched bemused as the imp happily re-worked knots of ever-increasing complexity. I guess everyone needs a hobby.

My stay at Rosie's was unremarkable. We had wangled a night in the main flat, Bastion and I in one bedroom and Oscar in another. Frogmatch insisted on patrolling the corridors whilst we slept. It seemed ridiculous to me that an eight-inch-tall imp could do anything in a real fight, but I knew better than to say so. Imps can be sensitive, and if I said the wrong thing my bodyguard would become my prankster and tormentor instead. Perhaps Frogmatch could tie any would-be attacker's shoelaces together.

The main apartment at Rosie's was far more spacious and opulent than the tiny hovel I'd stayed in last time, though I thought of the place with fondness since my stay there had saved my life. There was plenty of room for us all, even with the addition of pint-sized Frogmatch.

My skin crawls the whole time I am in the Common realm; I miss my magic like it is another limb. Bastion manfully distracted me to the best of his abilities – and the best of his abilities was very, very good.

The next morning I was eager to walk back through the portal, so I hustled downstairs at 6am after untying Frogmatch's artwork. I stalked through the portal and gave a happy sigh as my magic zinged back. We ate a leisurely breakfast at the café, watching the comings and goings of the Other folk. I nodded to those that I knew; there weren't many that I did not. I'd made it my business to network with all of the species and to make myself indispensable to them.

With my promise to Shirdal fulfilled, I had another outstanding vow: I had promised Krieg that I would find his mate. I'd told him that I would need time to design and make the potion, but that wasn't strictly true; I knew full well that Grimmy had such a potion in his pages because, as a teenager I'd been sorely tempted to use it. I hadn't because it had involved bloodletting, and if Mum had found out she would have been furious. Knowing a little more about Dad and his background, I could understand why. She would have been terrified that I'd slide down the slippery slope to black-witch territory.

I couldn't recall the full potion but I remembered that most of the ingredients were commonplace. I'd have to ask Grimmy for the details but I knew that I needed some milk thistle and bupleurum, both of which I was fresh out of having used the former in Ria's potion and the latter in Shirdal's final-defence potion.

After breakfast, we headed to the car. I opened the door but Frogmatch didn't hop in. 'I'm going to follow the vampyr,' he said firmly, braced for an argument.

'Which vampyr?' I asked.

'Voltaire. He knows more than he's telling us, Ellie, oath or no.'

'And what about your tail?' I asked archly. 'If he catches you following him, I've no doubt he'll chop it off as punishment.'

'I won't be enchanted a second time,' he groused. 'He won't see me coming.'

'It's a bad idea,' I stated firmly.

He grinned impishly at me. 'I disagree. And unless you really do consider me your slave, I have the free will to determine where I go and what I do.'

My mouth dropped open. 'Of course I don't consider you a slave!'

'Good. Off I go, then. I'll be in touch.' His red skin flashed as he scurried away. Try as I might, after a second I could no longer spot him. Vampyrs can phase, darting in one shadow and darting out of another. I had no idea how Frogmatch thought he could possibly find and then keep up with Voltaire.

Sighing, I turned back to the car. 'The Spice Shoppe, please,' I instructed Oscar as I slid onto the seat. I'd get all the ingredients that I could; if I needed more, I'd get one of the acolytes to run out for them.

I turned to Bastion. 'Can you reach out to Krieg? We need an appointment to get his blood for the mate potion.'

He frowned. 'Won't it be sufficient if he drops off a vial?'

I shook my head. 'This is a promise I've made. I'm not running the risk that it goes wrong because Krieg doesn't give me enough blood, or something like that. It needs to be gifted willingly, too. I don't want someone else drawing it in case Krieg begrudges it. After we've been to the shop, we'll swing by and get the blood. I can knock up the potion, deliver it, and then focus all my energy on this necromancer who keeps pissing me off.' And killing people.

Bastion pulled out his phone and started dialling while I opened my laptop and logged in remotely to the Coven's network. I fired off a couple of emails, pleased with how well things were running in the face of so much adversity.

By the time we arrived at The Spice Shoppe, Bastion had secured us an appointment with Krieg. Outside were two men – wizards, I guessed by the way the second one was casually juggling three cans with the IR. A Common realmer would see the man juggling but in reality his hands were still.

Bastion gave the two men the side eye and they bowed respectfully before scuttling back and giving him wide berth. It was weird to see his deadly reputation in action, especially when I knew what a sweetie he was.

I bustled around the shop. It was my happy place; the instant I walked in I was assaulted by an array of scents that took me back to long potion-brewing sessions with Mum. She had always been far more into her runes than her potions, but she'd made sure to encourage my love for them.

We'd come to The Spice Shoppe for as long as I could remember, back when it was owned by Old Man Jones. He'd died when I was young, so I couldn't remember his full name, but I remembered his smile and his blue twinkling eyes. He'd encouraged my love of potions too, sneaking extra ingredients into my shopping bag.

I wondered if there'd been a Young Jones or a Mrs Jones to mourn him. I'd been sad when he died, though I'd brushed off his death quickly in the way that children do. He'd seemed so *old,* though with hindsight I realised he was probably only in his sixties. He'd seemed ancient to young me, and now I felt ancient in turn.

I pulled myself out of memory lane and focused on the matter at hand as I zoomed around the store gathering the ingredients I needed. I indulged myself in a few that I didn't need but I couldn't quite resist as well. As usual, when I approached the till my shopping basket was overly full.

Henry, the shop assistant, had the triangle of the Other realm on his forehead. Angry red spots were dotted across his cheeks, but despite them he was a handsome lad. I could see why Ria was so taken with him.

'Hello, Coven Mother,' he greeted me respectfully. He looked around. Ascertaining that we were alone – bar

Bastion – he continued, 'Have you heard from Ria? I'm getting really worried.'

'They're just having an extended holiday,' I reassured him. 'Taking an unplugged break.'

'Ria would never go this long without talking to me.' He frowned. 'I'm her soulmate. We're going to get married.'

Goddess save me from young love. I smiled. 'I'm sure she'll be back before we know it,' I said confidently. 'She'll be glad to know she's missed.' Like Henry, Ria was tempestuous. In her youth she'd been wildly erratic at times, and she had darkened my office door frequently, for one infraction or another. But as she'd hit her teen years, she had found her stride. She had thankfully matured into the lovely young woman that Henry was currently obsessed with.

'It's like my right arm is missing,' he complained morosely. 'I'm incomplete without her.'

I pressed my lips together and fixed him with a stare. 'Henry, nobody needs anybody to complete them. You are a person in your own right. Your love interest doesn't complete you, they *complement* you.'

'I do like being told my hair is nice,' Henry conceded.

'Complement, not compliment.'

'What?'

I shook my head. 'Never mind. Just ring these through,' I sighed.

Bastion laughed quietly in my ear. 'You tried.'

'More fool me,' I grumped.

As usual, when my bags were packed, John slid out of his office to greet me. He gave a deferential bow before making a point of looking over my purchases. 'You have an excellent eye, Coven Mother. You've picked out the finest specimens.'

'As always, there are only the finest specimens to be found here.'

'You're too kind, Coven Mother, too kind.' He bobbed his bow again and touched his hand to his heart.

I cleared my throat awkwardly. 'Thank you for coming to Edinburgh – for coming to my aid.'

John grew serious and his professional customer-fronting smile faded. 'It was my honour to come to your assistance. Should you have need of me in the future, I will do it again without hesitation.'

I smiled. 'Thank you, John, I appreciate that.'

'Let me help you with your purchases.' He lifted the box and carried it out to the car. 'Footwell?' he asked.

'Please,' I confirmed.

I suddenly felt nervous. The last time I'd been here, someone had chucked a fireball at me. My car had been wrecked and Oscar had lain in a pool of his own blood. For a heartbeat, I was in that moment, filled with terror and fear.

John met my eyes. 'It won't happen again, Coven Mother,' he all-but growled fiercely. 'You have my word. An attack outside my shop! Unthinkable. I've hired wizard guards.' He gestured at the two men loitering by the open door, one of whom was the IR juggler we'd seen earlier.

I raised an eyebrow. I hadn't seen a request for further employees through the Coven. 'Paid for by you?' I queried briskly.

'Yes, Coven Mother. No need to bother the Coven's coffers for this.'

My phone blared and an unfamiliar number showed up. I frowned. 'Excuse me, John.'

'Of course.'

I swiped to answer the call.

Chapter 28

'There's been another attack.' Charlize's tone was brisk in my ear but even so my heart thundered.

My grip tightened on the phone. 'Is Mum okay?'

'She's fine.' Her voice turned rueful. 'It turns out all these paintings she's been doodling are rife with runes. That's why she was so prescriptive about where they were placed. She had thoroughly warded the property and the paintings lit up like a Christmas tree. The assailants couldn't get in – more's the pity.' She muttered the last part under her breath; she was clearly fixing for a fight.

'Thank the Goddess,' I breathed. 'Who tried to attack her?'

'Vampyrs controlled by a necromancer. They threw themselves against the walls, trying to phase in, and an earth elemental triggered a local earthquake. Nothing we couldn't handle.'

Fury bubbled up inside me. First the fire elemental and now this. Unfortunately there are mercenary rogues in every species. Still, it gave us something new to look into. This necro witch was beginning to test my patience.

'How did they locate my mum?' I demanded.

'Unknown, but items belonging to her were left in the care home. I suspect her location was scryed.'

I shook my head. Realising Charlize couldn't see me, I spoke aloud. 'No. Mum wouldn't have painted wards and not included an anti-scrying rune for privacy.' Dementia or time displacement or whatever it was, if she had the wherewithal to paint ward runes I doubted she would forget the basics. They were instinctive, like breathing.

I frowned. 'She didn't have any protective potions to paint the wards with!'

'No. She used her blood.'

My mouth dropped open. After all her dire warnings about blood work, she'd opened a vein or two to paint her runes. Mother, thou art a hypocrite.

'If she wasn't scryed then maybe there's a mole?' Charlize's tone was grim.

'A mole,' I confirmed. 'The simplest explanation is often the right one.' I sighed. I had emailed the Coven Council after the attack on Mum's care home. Obviously,

I hadn't said where she'd been moved to, but maybe it had been enough for someone to start to track her down. 'Are you moving my mother to another location?' I asked.

'Yes, we are moving imminently.'

'I'll come and rune the car you're travelling in,' I said, even though metal holds runes about as well as a sieve holds water.

'Not necessary,' she responded briskly. 'She's flying in the sun via Griffin Air.' She used the same term her father had. 'No shadows up there. I'll confirm once we're safely settled in the new venue.'

She rang off before I could point out that there could be other airborne dangers. Being a griffin, though, I guessed she knew all about aerial risks and she wouldn't appreciate me teaching a snake how to slither. I turned to Bastion. 'Mum was attacked.'

He nodded grimly. 'I heard the call. Do you want to go and see her?'

I did, desperately, but she was in the middle of her relocation and I had an appointment with Krieg. 'No, it's fine. Charlize is moving her. We'll go when she's settled. I don't want to upset her even more.'

As promised, John had placed my shopping in the front footwell of the car and Oscar was sitting in the driver's seat with the engine running. I'd have to tell him what had happened and give him the same option Bastion had just given me.

I slid into the car. 'Mum's been attacked. She's fine, but they're moving her. It turns out she'd painted wards into all of her paintings.' The words spilled out of me hastily so I could reassure Oscar quickly before panic set in.

Oscar gave a faint smile. 'That's my Luna. Even when she's down she's not out.'

'Do you want to go and see her?'

He turned to look at me. 'And where would I go to?'

I had no idea where they were relocating her. Ever-practical Oscar had a good point. 'I don't know,' I admitted.

Oscar's jaw was working. 'We have to trust the griffins to keep her safe,' he said finally. 'You have an appointment with Krieg and I'm not letting you stroll into the vipers' nest without me.'

The 'again' was unspoken but I heard it clearly. I nodded, like I had expected no less. 'To Krieg's, then.'

I buckled my seatbelt and the car moved off smoothly. As we drove, Bastion reached out and linked his fingers through mine, drawing a smile from me despite my anxiety. I let him feel how happy that simple touch made me, even with everything else in the world going to heck in a handcart. His answering wash of emotion took my breath away.

I was too much of a coward to disentangle all my confused feelings, save for acknowledging that they were pleasant ones. He cared, and that was enough.

It would have to be because I was too broken to offer more.

Chapter 29

'So, you need my blood,' Krieg stated coolly.

'Yes, for the mate potion.'

His brow furrowed as he looked at me impatiently. 'And why would you not let me simply send you a sample?'

'I need more than a vial and it needs to be drawn carefully. You have to give it willingly. I won't have the potion fail because you couldn't fit me in for five minutes in your oh-so-busy day,' I snapped.

The attack on Mum had made me anxious, and whenever I feel worried I lash out; it's better than letting others see you are vulnerable. Nevertheless, I took a deep breath and tried to dial it back; Krieg wasn't someone I wanted to piss off.

'May I?' I asked, more evenly. I drew out my athame and my bloodwork bowl.

Krieg shook his head. 'You're not cutting me with that piddling thing,' he sneered.

He reached up to one of the tusks that protruded from his head, slid his arm down it and sliced the flesh of his forearm. He grabbed my bowl and held the wound over it, letting blood drip into the wooden vessel. He'd cut deeply and rather than a small drip it was a steady river. In seconds, I had more than enough.

I pulled out a healing potion and a paintbrush and hastily painted on *hagalaz* for injury and *sowilo* for health. I pulled my magic through the runes and watched them light up. His flesh knitted together effortlessly, leaving not a hint of the deep gash that had been there moments before.

'Is the potion ready?' Krieg asked abruptly, not acknowledging my healing.

You're welcome. 'Not yet, but it will be. I'll do it later today.'

'I will return with you to the Coven,' he said abruptly.

'That's not necessary. It will take a significant while to brew it.'

'Nonetheless, I will attend.'

It occurred to me that once I'd brewed his potion, he'd have no reason not to fulfil his original contract and kill me – but he had given me his word that he wouldn't and I honestly believed him. Ogres are obsessed with their word and their honour. Besides, I had Bastion by my side; even Krieg would think twice before crossing him, even if he were willing to cross me.

I outlined my terms. 'You can attend the Coven with one companion of your choice. Both of you must remain in the reception area.'

'Five others,' he objected.

'Two.'

'Three.'

'Two, or I don't make the potion today,' I snarled. I was all out of patience and his bickering was getting under my skin.

He glared before nodding. He rose fluidly. 'Hanlon, Maktel,' he called. 'You're with me.'

Two ogres peeled out of the trees. Talk about being at one with nature; I hadn't even *seen* the horned creatures until they'd wanted me to.

They were amongst the tallest ogres I'd ever seen and they gave me a moment's pause. My mind flashed back to the ogre swinging his mace towards my face in the underground city. Benji had stopped him. I missed my golem and that made my heart ache with an unfamiliar sensation. Having friends had some real downsides.

Krieg took a separate car to the Coven tower and I noted with interest that he drove himself. He seemed like a bit of a control freak – not that I could throw stones on that score.

I took a small amount of pleasure in leaving the ogres to cool their heels downstairs whilst I went up to my apartment. It was my favourite time: potion time. As we reached his floor, Oscar hesitated.

'Go,' I urged. 'Have a break. I won't be in any danger here.' The memory of the wreck of my bedroom after a bomb had exploded in it shone before my eyes. Okay, I *probably* wouldn't be in any danger here.

'The ogres—' Oscar started.

'—are here to collect a potion. Nothing more.'

He was wrestling with his conscience. 'Do you have an address for Luna?' he asked Bastion. 'I want to see her. I just need to know she's okay.'

Bastion nodded, pulled out his phone, scrolled to a message then showed it to Oscar. Oscar typed the address into his own phone. 'I won't be long,' he promised. 'I'll be back before the potion is finished.'

'It's okay. Go, send her my love – if the time is right,' I said.

He nodded.

'And ask her—'

'—about the code for the CD. I know. I will.' We shared a small smile and he walked back down towards the garage.

Bastion looked after him with a faint frown. 'And that's why he shouldn't be your bodyguard. He's leaving you with the ogres to go and check on your mum.'

'The ogres aren't breathing over me. Besides, I have you.'

A warm feeling rolled over me as he met my eyes. 'Yes,' he said. 'You have me.'

Chapter 30

I stroked my finger down Grimmy's spine and a small tingle ran through me as he awakened. His pages flipped, giving me the impression of someone stretching and yawning. 'Why, good morning, Miss Amber – or should I say good afternoon?'

'Good afternoon, Grimmy,' I responded after a quick glance at my watch revealed it was gone midday. Time flies when you're having fun and/or meeting with ogre kings.

'What can I assist you with this fine day?'

The day was indeed fine and sun was streaming into my bedroom. His words reminded me that I hadn't drawn my curtains so I hurriedly attended to them. I was in too much haste to get this potion done; I mustn't get sloppy. No one could learn of Grimmy's existence or he'd be a target for theft or destruction, and I wanted neither of those to come to pass.

When I'd taken him to Edinburgh with me, I'd toyed with the idea of using anything I could find in his pages to save Abigay but I knew she wouldn't have let me. Benji had taken charge of Grimmy and encased my grimoire inside his body, where Grimmy had still been when Benji was shut down. When Benji handed him back, I'd feared Grimmy might have suffered some damage but luckily I'd seen no evidence. Even so, I was keeping a watchful eye on him; somehow he did seem a little different.

'I need the potion for finding someone's mate,' I explained

'How very pedestrian.' Grimmy sighed, unimpressed with my request. He opened the bartering. 'Four weeks.'

I laughed. 'I'm not giving you four weeks of my life force for that tiny spell. I'm ninety percent sure I remember the potion anyway,' I lied smoothly. 'An hour.'

'An hour?' he spluttered. 'Why, Miss Amber, you wound me! It is almost like you *want* me to wither into nothingness.'

'Not at all! I value you, Grimmy, you know that. There's no other tome like you.' A little flattery never hurt.

'An hour!' he continued to splutter. 'You certainly do *not* value me, Miss Amber! A day and not a moment less!'

That was actually an okay deal. I hoped it was a rubbish day that our agreement would take from me, rather than a good one. 'A day,' I agreed. 'Done and done, payment on successful completion of the potion.' It was a small price for getting the ogres off my back and the contract to kill me cancelled. Certain death versus a day off my life: yes, it would do.

'You wound me with your lack of trust.' There was a pause then he drew in a sharp breath. 'Miss Amber! You have a familiar! I see the bond as clear as day! Oh my, why you let me blather on when you had such joyous news I do not know. A familiar! What is it? Oh, I bet it is a cat like the one resting beside me in your safe! Is it a cat?'

'Kind of,' I said, thinking of Bastion in all of his glory. He was half-lion after all, which was a big cat...

'Do not keep me in suspense a moment longer!' Grimmy pleaded.

I sighed. He wasn't going to like this; he'd been made in a time when Ante-Crea sentiment was rife. 'It's a griffin.'

The silence was deafening. When he finally spoke, his tone was disbelieving. 'A griffin? How can that be? I have never in all my days heard of a familiar bonding with a *creature*.' His voice dropped to a whisper. 'You are cursed, child.'

Gee, thanks Grimmy. Don't pull your punches on my account. 'I am no child, nor am I cursed,' I said firmly, hands on my hips. 'I am a witch. And I am honoured and *proud* to be bonded to Bastion.'

'A creature of death,' Grimmy whispered. 'No good can come of this, Miss Amber. None at all.'

'What would you have me do?' I asked snarkily. 'Sever the bond?'

'Goddess, no!' The response was immediate and gratifying.

'Then what do you suggest?'

'I do not know,' he replied slowly. 'But it is a troubling and mystifying development. A bond with a creature. What a thing!'

At that, the light faded from him and he slumped back onto the bed; apparently Grimmy was done wasting his life on my troubles. The book didn't close, however, but remained open at the potion I needed. I recognised the spikey writing that I'd studied once before: it was an old ancestor's potion.

I didn't want to heave Grimmy around my flat, so I took a picture of the two pages. I turned to the next one and it was blank, as were the rest of his pages: he only showed you what you'd bargained for. Having secured the potion – for now and always – I closed him and placed him back in the safe.

I felt a jolt as I saw my stuffed cat sitting there. It was a gift from Aunt Abigay. She had been ripped away from life, and from me, far too soon. As there was no one to see, I grasped the cat and gave her a quick hug. How I wished I could hug Abigay. I hadn't done it enough in life and, though I tried hard not to drag regret around with me, that omission stung a little.

I placed the toy cat back on her shelf and swung the safe shut with a clang. I wished that the sound was less ominous. It felt like a dark foreshadowing of what was to come.

Chapter 31

I was sweating over the potion that was simmering away in a bronze cauldron even before I increased the flames underneath it to make it really boil. I was brewing in a small cauldron, but it was one of my most powerful receptacles.

I pushed back a sticky strand of hair that had fallen loose from my braid. With a sigh, I grabbed another clip to keep it out of my face and out of the potion. A stray hair from me and the whole thing would be ruined. I didn't fancy keeping Krieg hanging around much longer; he'd already been waiting for more than six hours. Still, the potion had to be right and the ingredients wouldn't be rushed.

I crushed the milk thistle and waited for the temperature to rise. The brew was bubbling vigorously and if I waited too long to turn it down, it would be ruined. It had to be timed to perfection. The thermometer was in the cauldron but in truth I didn't need it to tell me that the potion was ready for me to add the milk thistle. I poured it in deftly with one hand whilst stirring with the other. I continued to stir with my right hand as my left hand doused the flames.

I kept one eye on the temperature of the liquid. When it hit ninety degrees exactly, I carefully lifted the cauldron and placed it in an ice bath. The cauldron hissed in protest at the shock of the cold, and steam rose. I smiled smugly. Perfect. Now for the final ingredient – and Krieg wanted to be present when I added that.

I walked back through my office and into the living room. The atmosphere was tense. Krieg was sprawled on my sofa with his two henchmen standing behind him on sentry duty. Bastion's body was rigid. Violence stirred in the air.

I frowned at Krieg. 'You were supposed to wait in reception.'

'I did,' he growled. 'For five and a half hours. Then I grew impatient.'

'Did I give you the impression that it was a quick potion?' I asked, exasperated.

'You did not,' he admitted.

'I told you I would summon you,' I huffed. 'But since you're here, you may as well come in.' I paused. 'Just you,' I clarified. His guards stiffened.

Krieg nodded once. 'Fine, but the griffin stays here with them.'

'Amber...' Bastion started.

'Stay here,' I ordered firmly. 'Keep an eye on these two. Krieg has given his word he won't harm me. If he goes back on his word then you have my permission to slice him into sashimi.'

Bastion's jaw tightened and I felt his anxiety. I tried to reassure him, but I was still a novice at this bond thing so I had no idea whether it worked or not. I kept the bond as open as possible so he could feel that I was working calmly and nothing more.

Krieg followed me into my office then into my no-longer-so-secret laboratory behind it. I checked the temperature of the potion and moved the cauldron to my tripod stand, then I went to the fridge. I'd covered the bowl that was filled with Krieg's blood with clingfilm and placed it in there. If I'd known that Krieg was going to insist on waiting, I would have drawn the blood fresh rather than risking spilling it in my car on the way home. But there you go.

I peeled back the sticky film and poured the cold blood into the cooling potion. I grimaced a little as I spotted a few clots; they weren't a problem but they made my stomach turn. As the dark blood dripped in, the potion started to swirl. Slowly it shifted from a sludgy brown colour to a crystal-clear potion, as clear as water.

'Lean forward,' I instructed Krieg. 'At first you'll only see yourself reflected in the potion, but then it will shimmer and show you your mate.'

Krieg's hands curled into fists at his side but that was only indication that he was tense. His face was calm. I made a mental note never to play poker with him.

He leaned forward over the clear liquid. His reflection stared back at him, then it shimmered and the potion turned pearlescent. His image faded and another vision replaced it. 'Oh heck,' I said aloud as I saw who was staring back at him, a hint of defiance in her gaze.

'You know her?' Krieg asked. He tried to say it casually, but I wasn't buying it.

'Stacey Wise. She's an inspector in the Connection.' I'd only met her briefly, but she'd struck me as ballsy. She'd need to be if she was going to get hot and heavy with the ogre king.

'Stacey,' he repeated reverently, a small smile tugging at his mouth.

'She works in and around Chester and Liverpool.'

'Then that is where I shall go.' He pushed back from the potion. 'She's a wizard?'

'I assume so, though I haven't witnessed any magic from her.' I paused and asked an impertinent question. 'Were you expecting an ogre?'

'No,' he admitted. 'I've travelled up and down this country and across Europe. I've met with many of the ruling ogres and their people, but no one has drawn my gaze.'

'Will it cause problems for you? A human-creature relationship?'

He smiled, and there was nothing friendly about it. 'Only temporarily.' I could hear the subtext clearly: anyone who made it an issue would catch a sudden case of death. I wondered what Inspector Wise would think about that.

I cleared my throat. 'I take it that you accept that the potion has been made to your satisfaction and, as such, my end of the deal has been upheld?'

Krieg nodded once. 'I do.'

'Then you will permanently cancel the contract?'

'I will.' He paused. 'I will put a permanent ban on killing you. Obviously I can lift it if you piss me off, but for now you are safe from all ogres in the UK.'

I was surprised by the weight of relief and gratitude I felt. 'Thank you,' I murmured.

'Thank you for freely telling me her name and location,' he said stiffly. 'Good day, Miss DeLea.'

I bowed lower than I would usually have done and saw him smile a little. He made his way out of my lab. No doubt we both felt like we'd got the best side of the bargain. With the contract out on me cancelled, it was only the black witches and the necromancer I needed to concern myself with. Piece of cake.

When I walked into my living room it was ogre free. Krieg had wasted no time making tracks, eager to either connect with his mate or to leave my Coven; both were fine with me.

Bastion had boiled the kettle. 'Tea?' he asked lightly.

I hesitated. The last time I'd had a cup of tea, it had been poisoned. However, I didn't want Becky to have any sort of long-term effect on me and I trusted Bastion implicitly so I nodded. 'Yes, please. That would be nice.'

If he was surprised by response, I didn't feel it through our bond; rather, I felt a tendril of something I'd have called pride. He was proud of me? That felt surprisingly nice. I hadn't had anyone other than my mother, Oscar or Aunt Abigay feel proud of me before. There is something possessive about a sense of pride, and I found that I quite liked the idea of Bastion feeling possessive about me.

He made the tea and brought my cup over to me. His mug had a picture of a unicorn on it and said: *Back the hell up, sparkle tits. Today is not the day. I will shank you with my horn.*

I snorted with amusement. 'Now, I *know* that's not one of mine. I knew you'd been expanding my collection! Have you been amusing yourself with buying mugs, sparkle tits?'

He flashed me a grin and his pecs did a little dance under his shirt, making my chuckle transform into a full-blown guffaw.

I examined my own mug: was it an old one or a Bastion one? It said: *I'm not an early bird or a night owl, I'm some form of permanently exhausted pigeon.* I laughed at that. A Bastion one, for sure, and it wasn't wrong. I burned both ends of the candle, but who had time for sleep? After all, you could rest when you were dead.

My phone rang before I had taken my first sip of tea. It was Voltaire. I took a deep breath. I was tired after spending a six hours making a complex potion and I did *not* want to be going to some sort of black-witch auction just now.

I swiped to answer. 'DeLea.' My voice was terse.

'I have something of yours,' he groused. 'I'll dump him tonight in the shadows by the Coven tower.'

'Is he in one piece?' I asked calmly.

'For now. He's an annoying little prick so my answer might change.' He cleared his throat. 'The soul auction is tomorrow night. I'll send further details once I know them. I trust you have a disguise ready.' He rang off.

I glared at the phone. 'Bye-bye,' I said to the disconnect tone. 'Nice chatting to you.'

'You know that your passive-aggressive sarcasm works better when they can hear you?' Bastion quipped.

'He is such a jerk.' I sipped my tea to calm my nerves; it was like manna from the heavens and I gave a happy sigh. 'Oh tea, I have missed you.'

'I think I'm jealous,' Bastion laughed.

'Don't be. I make better noises than that for you.' I winked.

He grinned broadly. 'You do. Drink up so we can make some more.'

I do not react well to orders, but this was one that I could get behind. I drank up.

Chapter 32

Oscar joined Bastion and me for breakfast. 'How was Mum?' I asked over a blueberry muffin and a cappuccino. I already knew the answer, since Oscar had brought me the blueberry muffin and the cappuccino.

'She knew me.' He hesitated. 'She thought you were eight so I didn't mention you much. I'm sorry.'

I ignored the sting that brought; my turn to be forgotten, then. 'That's fine,' I said brusquely, even though it wasn't. 'The codes?'

He shook his head. 'She didn't have a clue what I was talking about. Possibly she made the CD later in her life. She got distressed when I pressed her so I left it alone. I'm sorry.'

'Don't be,' I said firmly. 'You did the right thing.' I looked at Bastion as I said the next words. 'But I think it leaves me with no choice. I need to break the clearing on my mind.'

'Bambi,' Bastion growled. 'No! It's been in place for too long. It will hurt like a bitch.'

'I can handle a little bit of pain.' I can't, I'm a total wuss, but I lied anyway. 'We can't go to this auction tonight and not have every weapon in our arsenal. What if my dad is there and I could recognise him? I can't go in ignorant. This is something I have to do.' I wasn't asking for his permission.

He felt my determination as much as I felt his sudden resignation and I smiled at him as he accepted my choice.

'Who will you get to break it?' Oscar asked.

Now that was a loaded question. Before all of this, the answer would have been Meredith without a doubt. She was my little protégée, but with her ensconced in the Other Circus my choices were limited. Hannah, perhaps, or Jeb or Ethan.

I pulled out my phone and checked the Coven diary. Hannah and Ethan were both out on jobs. Jeb then. 'Jeb.'

Bastion protested, 'I don't like him.'

My cheeks warmed a little. 'Because he ... *likes* me?' It was only at Bastion's insistence that I'd realised that dear, sweet Jeb fancied me a little. I didn't reciprocate his feelings, of course – he was far too young for me. Plus, I just wasn't into hero worship. I'm a human, not a Goddess, and in any event the only way to move from the top of the pedestal is to fall.

'Maybe,' Bastion admitted begrudgingly.

I shrugged. 'We need someone we can trust. I trust Jeb.'

Bastion's lips pressed into a thin line but he nodded. 'Fine.'

I almost told him I wasn't asking for his permission, but I recognised it as a self-sabotaging impulse so I swallowed it down.

Frogmatch piped up, making me jump. 'I've been thinking. Should I hide myself in the Coven, Ellie? I could go undercover like a spy. I could sneak through your Coven and see who is doing what, maybe get some clues about any black witches.' He leaned forward eagerly, willing me to say yes to his 007 dreams.

Voltaire had been true to his word; late last night Frogmatch had been chucked out of the shadows near the Coven tower. He'd had very little to report, save that Voltaire had not harmed him. Sending Frogmatch on further reconnaissance missions when he'd failed his first one so spectacularly seemed a risk, but I doubted that Frogmatch would listen if I said no.

For all he'd sworn fealty to me, he seemed incredibly independent. To be honest, I preferred it that way. I felt awkward having an indentured servant; it was only one step away from slavery and there was enough of that in modern society without me perpetuating it. Besides, I couldn't see any particular downsides – as long as he didn't get caught again. In fact, it could be downright useful.

'Go for it Frogmatch. Keep yourself unseen and report anything suspicious immediately.'

He snapped off a cheeky salute and disappeared from view.

'Keeping him busy?' Bastion asked with amusement.

'He's not pranking us if he has a mission.'

'Smart.'

I messaged Jeb and requested his presence in my room to break a mind clearing, though I didn't specify on whom. He answered in the affirmative and said he would retrieve some revelation potion from the Coven's store unless I had some to hand. It was one I often had handy, but I'd used the last recently and hadn't had time to replenish it. I told him as much, and he said he'd be there in fifteen minutes.

I turned to Bastion. 'Can you find out who is acting as the Seer High Priestess after Melva's death? I have "Ellie Tron's" cloak but we'll need a cloak of shadows for you.'

Seer-bespelled artefacts are expensive and rare. We'd need to go straight to the top to get Bastion a cloak that would hide all of his features, but I was confident that the new High Priestess, whoever she was, would want Melva's killer found and dealt with so she'd oblige. The murdering vampyr had been under a necromancer's control and I was hunting that necromancer.

'I can find out,' Bastion confirmed easily. There were no secrets from him. He just needed to find a talkative Seer and coax them or ask Shirdal if he knew who was in charge. Bastion's power to coax should have made me feel nervous but oddly it didn't. If I'd learned anything in the past few weeks, it was that he was incredibly honourable. Sure, his code of honour might not line up with the law, but he certainly wasn't the black-hearted killer I'd once thought he was.

Chapter 33

Bastion went off to make enquiries about the High Priestess whilst Oscar and I washed the dishes together. I preferred to wash, he preferred to dry: it was the perfect partnership. My kitchen had a double sink, one full of hot water and soapy suds and one full of cold water to wash the soap off again. I rinsed another bowl and passed it to Oscar to dry. We'd found a rhythm over the years and I wondered if he felt like Bastion's arrival into our lives had thrown that off.

'I—' I began.

'Amber—' he started at the same time.

'You go first,' I said with a laugh.

'Things with Bastion – they've … developed?' He seemed as uncomfortable talking about it as I was.

My neck heated and then my face followed suit. 'Erm, yes. I like him.'

'I do too.' Oscar assured me. 'He's a good man.'

'I think so.'

'He makes you happy?'

I thought about it then nodded. Our relationship might seem odd to some because essentially I was Bastion's boss. Each day I decided where we went and what we did, and he came along to protect me. That power disparity might have been difficult for some, but he had enough wealth never to work again. He didn't need me for the money any more than I needed his money.

And he was powerful in a way that I wasn't. He could coax and he could kill. He was respected and feared by almost everyone. I might be the boss but that was only because he was allowing me to be. And I might order him around for eighteen hours a day but he was happy to be the boss in the bedroom – we were both happy with that arrangement. Though that wasn't something I wanted to confess to my pseudo-father.

I cleared my throat. 'He makes me very happy. It just ... works.'

Oscar searched my face before smiling. 'I'm glad, Am. And your mother would be, too. I think it might have taken her a while to get her head around it, but ultimately she would have been happy for you.'

'I know she would.' I hated that we were talking in the past tense. I managed a tight smile. 'Thanks for the chat.'

He reddened slightly. 'We don't need to talk about protection, right?'

My cheeked flared red. 'He's my protector,' I responded, wilfully misunderstanding his comment.

'That's not what I was talking about.'

'I know and I'm deliberately misinterpreting so we don't have to discuss condoms. I'm forty-two, Oscar.'

'Right.' He cleared his throat. 'I just needed to be sure that you're being sensible. You've always said you don't want kids.'

'I don't,' I said firmly. 'Bastion and I have discussed it and he's okay with that. He has Charlize, after all.'

'And are you ready to become a step-parent?'

I grinned a little and nudged him with my shoulder. 'If I've learned anything from Disney, it's that all stepmothers are evil. So no, not yet.' I sobered. 'We've really only just started this thing. I don't want to put the horse before the cart.'

'The cart before the horse. The horse always pulls the cart.'

'All right, Mr Equestrian. Not all of us know all things equine.'

He was laughing at me. 'Most people know how horses and carts work.'

'I've never been on a horse and cart ride, so sue me.'

There was a knock at the door and Oscar went to get it. Jeb came in wearing his backpack. 'Who am I runing?' he asked good-naturedly.

'Me.'

His eyebrows rose. 'Who dared to clear *you?*'

'My mum,' I admitted. 'When I was a kid.'

'This'll hurt like a bitch, Coven Mother,' he warned. 'The clearing has been in place for a long time.'

'I'm aware,' I responded drily. As a healer and rune mistress, I knew far more about both subjects than Jeb, who was a mid-level runist at best.

'Sorry, I didn't mean to teach you how to stir a cauldron,' Jeb muttered with an apologetic glance.

He set down his backpack and pulled out his paintbrush and the black sludgy revelation potion, then pulled on purple gloves. Most potions don't require the gloves and we use them for show, but not the revelation potion. You do *not* want to get that stuff on your skin unless you have the protection of the runes.

Jeb often brought his familiar with him when he did rune work but I couldn't see the black rabbit. 'Where's Jessica?' I asked curiously.

'She's a having a run in the Coven's garden.'

'Who is Jessica?' Bastion asked as he joined us.

'Jeb's familiar, a black lop-eared rabbit.'

Bastion looked amused. 'You have your own Jessica Rabbit?'

'Living the dream,' Jeb joked with a wink.

'Clearly.' Bastion moved closer to me. 'I have the information we need and I've set up a meet after we're done here with breaking the clearing.'

'She won't be doing anything after the clearing is broken,' Jeb interjected. 'She'll be a miserable mess.'

'Thanks,' I said drily.

'You know what I mean.'

Bastion sat down next me. 'She's stronger than she looks.'

'Hey!' I protested. 'I look strong.'

He smiled and pressed a kiss to my forehead. 'You're very tough,' he agreed, but I felt his amusement. He thought I was about as strong as a feather. I narrowed my eyes at him.

He backpedalled. 'You *are* strong in mind and spirit. You're the most determined person I've ever met, but physically you probably couldn't bench-press twenty kilograms. Which is fine, because I can bench-press six hundred kilograms.'

'Am I supposed to be impressed?'

A smile pulled at his lips. 'Yes.'

'Ah. Well then, I am. Very.'

He laughed. Jeb was watching the two of us, his eyes dark; all hints of humour had slid from his face. Oops. He'd just realised that Bastion and I were a couple. I cleared my throat; it was time to get back to business. 'Shall we?' I gestured to my forehead.

'Of course,' Jeb said tightly. 'Prepare yourself.'

I closed my eyes but, as it turned out, no amount of visualising the brace position could prepare me for what was coming.

Chapter 34

I focused on the memories I wanted to be revealed. *Memories of my father.* Jeb painted thick cold runes on my forehead. The moment the revelation potion touched my head, flashes started to come to me.

My father was cuddling me. 'It's okay,' he murmured, kissing my elbow. 'There, all better now.'

Tears formed behind my eyelids and my heart stuttered. He didn't *seem* evil.

'Shaun!' my mother laughed, as he tickled her. 'Stop it! The potion needs the ara root adding now!'

My father fixed his green eyes on me. 'Well then ... I need a new victim.' I squealed with laughter as I ran away.

I had his eyes; my hair was red to his blond but our eyes were the same, right down to their shape. When I looked in the mirror, he'd be staring back at me.

As Jeb filled in the triangles on my forehead, the memories came thicker and faster, more vivid than any I'd ever had before. Family picnics, outings to the park, a trip to the aquarium. Reading with him under a blanket fort by torchlight, studying the stars with a telescope, going swimming in a pool with waves and slides.

His name was Shaun Bolton and he was a great father. I had absolutely zero doubt that he'd loved me with all of his heart until Mum had kicked him out. I knew she'd had her reasons, but six-year-old me hadn't known them.

Ripping away the memories of my father had helped me deal with his supposed abandonment and I'd stopped caring that he'd gone. But Mum hadn't just taken a few memories away from me; she'd erased the whole relationship. Whatever my dad had done, it was hard to accept that her choice had been the right one.

Pain overwhelmed me, physical and emotional.

I opened my eyes. 'Stop,' I pleaded, but my plea was superfluous. Jeb was already cleaning the runes from my forehead. He studied me with open concern. I had just enough presence of mind to check him over too. Magic like this took its toll, but Jeb looked fine.

I relaxed, and let the pain take me. My vision tunnelled as I passed out.

Something cool touched my skin and I groaned in appreciation. My head was pounding; someone was banging a drum inside the confines of my skull. I opened my eyes and immediately regretted it as agonising pain lanced through me. I scrunched them shut. A low moan escaped my lips, not the good kind.

'I'm sorry, Bambi,' Bastion whispered. 'I know you're hurting. We have the Seer's meeting in twenty minutes.' He paused. 'I'll cancel it.'

'No!' I said forcefully, wincing at the sound of my voice. 'No,' I repeated, this time in a whisper. 'I'll be fine.'

'You won't be,' he said firmly. 'I know you're in pain.' He paused. 'I'm your familiar. I can send you energy like I did after the incident with Becky. Can I help with this? Will you let me take your pain? I tried while you were out, but I barely managed to touch the surface.'

I licked my parched lips, keeping my eyes closed as I debated. He could, but did I want him to? Of the two of us, I knew who I'd rather be incapacitated. ' I get migraines occasionally – I have some migraine medication in my bedside drawer. The meds might make me a bit woozy but they'll help. Get me paracetamol and ibuprofen, too.'

I still had my eyes tightly closed but I could hear the frown in his voice as he said, 'Should you take those together?'

'I'm a healer witch,' I sassed. 'I know about potion and drug interactions. That combination is fine. Give them to me. Now. Please.' I managed not to whimper the last word.

I heard him rooting around in the bedside drawer and deduced I was lying on my bed. Call me Sherlock Holmes. A moment later he pressed a cup to my lips. I took a sip of the water and held out my hand for pills. He passed me a few of them and I knocked them back. 'Can you carry me to the car?' I suggested. 'I'll be fine after these meds kick in.'

He didn't answer but his hands slid under my skirt and he cradled me gently to his chest. I'm not a skinny rake of a woman – I have meat on my bones – so it felt both surprising and thrilling to realise that he could carry me so effortlessly.

We descended the stairs and I felt the air around me cool as we entered the underground car park. Oscar was behind the wheel of the car. Bastion buckled me in but then wrapped his arms around me. I winced when the engine caught.

I dozed lightly as we drove; the pain was less intrusive when my eyes eventually peeled open, but it was still there. Goddess, it was really there. Bastion looked concerned. 'Oscar says I can help, so I'm going to help.' His tone brooked no argument. He wasn't asking for permission.

I nodded. 'A little, yes. Don't take it all. Better that both of us deal with a bit of a headache rather than having one of us totally incapacitated.'

I felt his relief and realised that he'd been expecting a fight. My head was pounding, even with all of the medicine coursing through my veins, and I was all out of arguments. I just wanted it not to hurt. I have many good attributes, but fortitude in the face of overwhelming pain isn't one of them. I let out a whimper that I couldn't stop.

Bastion drew a breath and I felt him tug on the bond between us. It felt weird, like skin being tugged under local anaesthetic. The pain started to fade.

'Enough.' I pulled back, physically and metaphorically. 'That's enough. I'm okay now, I can cope with this.' I could; I'd completed potions with full-blown focal migraines, blinking away shimmering lights and battling holes in my vision. This had been far worse than any migraine I'd experienced, but now it was down to pre-migraine pain levels I could, and would, cope.

I reached for the bond between us and felt that Bastion was in more pain than I was. He'd taken the lion's share of the agony. I hated that and loved him for it in equal measure. Crud. I *liked* him for it – it was *kind*. That was all.

'Thanks,' I murmured, even though it was still hard for me to acknowledge. 'You took too much, but thanks.'

I felt him shift aside the pain as if he could just ignore it. I had no doubt he'd had a lifetime of ignoring debilitating wounds; this was just a headache to him, a bad one but hardly life-threatening. With the pain split between the two of us, it was far more manageable than the agony I'd had to contend with alone. There was real truth in the saying that a burden shared was a burden halved.

He kissed my lips gently. 'Let's go, Bambi. We have a High Priestess to meet and a black auction to get to.'

Ugh. Don't remind me.

Chapter 35

I had been completely out of it, so it took me a moment to realise that we were walking into Melva's office. Nell was sitting at her desk, eyes red-rimmed and raw. She said nothing as I walked in: there was no quip, no barb, and I was surprised to realise that I missed it. She just picked up the phone and spoke quietly into it. 'Your 12pm is here.' A beat of silence. 'Yes, ma'am.' She hung up the phone and looked up. 'You can go in.'

Oscar led the way and Bastion pulled up the rear. As I walked past Nell, I laid a hand on her shoulder and gave it a light squeeze. It isn't often that we touch Other realmers – especially not the Seers – because if they choose to they can read you, your future and your hopes. It is an intimate thing to touch a Seer, something reserved for friends. Nell and I weren't that, but we weren't adversaries. Not any more.

Nell looked up at me and her eyes suddenly filled. She laid her hand on top of mine and gave it a light squeeze back. As her hand dropped away I let mine fall too. I didn't have any words to offer her, no empty platitudes to utter. Nothing would ease the loss of her boss and friend whom she'd served faithfully for more than a decade.

Melva had been kind, warm and universally liked. A necromancer had made a vampyr slide into her safe haven and murder her and now here I was, strolling into the same safe haven once more. This time it didn't feel so safe and I bet Nell felt the same.

I lifted my chin and walked in. I recognised the woman behind the desk, of course: I tried to know all the movers and shakers. Liyana had been full of promise for a while, but her hard edges had seen her relegated to the political sidelines. Now, apparently, people wanted hard edges; the Seers wanted to make it clear they weren't soft and they weren't kind. There was neither softness nor kindness in Liyana's gaze as she looked at me, her mouth a grim line.

Bastion had murmured to me before we walked in that Liyana had been made High Priestess earlier that day. Unlike the Coven Council, which dragged out every decision until it had been debated at length, the Seers were decisive. I guess knowing the future really helped with that.

'High Priestess Liyana, it is my honour to meet with you this day.' I touched my hand to my heart and bowed.

'It is indeed your honour,' she replied, studying me like a spider gazing at a fly. I was a nuisance, one to be eradicated.

My eyes narrowed. I was neither of those things, and if she thought she was a spider then she would soon learn that I was a scorpion. I ate spiders for breakfast. 'I have come to ask a boon,' I soldiered on.

'Bold of you, given that the last Seer you spoke to died whilst in your care.'

'Melva was not in my care.' I spoke carefully even as my temper spiked. 'Though I did go to great lengths to try and save her.'

'Yet you failed.' Her words were cold.

My gut clenched. How I hated that word, hated it even more because she was correct. I *had* failed. 'Yes,' I said simply.

'No,' Bastion growled. 'Amber did not fail. Melva herself said that it was her time. She had foreseen it and it could not be undone, no matter how hard we tried.'

'And did you try, *protector,* to save her?' Liyana sneered.

'I did,' Bastion confirmed.

Liyana lost some of her combative stance. She believed us – or at least she believed Bastion. 'What brings you before me?' she asked abruptly.

I doubted she'd appreciate me crawling around a pentagram so I got right to it. 'I need a bespelled cloak.'

'Why?'

'I'm hunting the necromancer that killed Melva. I want them dead. There's going to be a gathering of black witches at an auction of dark artefacts and we need to go to it.'

'Why?' she asked again. 'What will your presence do?' she sneered.

'We'll infiltrate the auction and we'll gather information to end the black witches.'

She barked a laugh. 'You and a griffin against the full might of the black Coven – and more black witches besides – gathered in one place?'

'You know about the black Coven?' My eyes narrowed.

'It is impossible to see the future without doing so.'

That wasn't good, not good at all. 'Do they win?' I asked, my heart pounding suddenly.

Liyana's mouth twisted in a caricature of a smile, 'Why, Amber DeLea, have you started to believe in prophecy?'

I glared. 'I've always believed in prophecy, I just don't like it. I don't want my actions to be anything but my own.

If you tell me my future is predestined, what is the point of life? I would simply be a marionette, strolling down the pre-set path made for me. What joy does that bring?'

'It is not the destination that matters but the journey itself,' she said sanctimoniously.

'If the journey is written in the stars then why bother?'

'Fool! There are hundreds of paths stretching before you, a million journeys to take.'

'Perhaps. But knowing about one of them sets it in stone.' I folded my arms. 'And that is why I don't like prophecy because it is trying to cajole me down one of many paths. If it succeeds, my future is set.'

She huffed in exasperation. 'It is not so ham-fisted as that. You fail to appreciate the intricacies and subtleties of a prophecy. If it is told to you at one time it may have one meaning, but told to you at another you might interpret it completely differently.'

I sighed and my head pounded a little more. 'Can we argue about the worth of prophecy another time? My head is aching and I need a Seer-bespelled cloak. I need it now. Name your price.' Revealing how much I needed the cloak was not my wisest negotiating move, but pain was making me blunder. I needed to gather my wits, which were scattered around me like rune stones clumsily tossed by an acolyte.

Liyana pursed her lips. 'A favour, Amber DeLea. Of my timing and choosing,' she said finally.

'One favour, but with the caveat that I will not assist you by act or omission in harming or killing another living being.'

'Done and done.'

'So mote it be.' I touched a hand to my aching temples.

'Witnessed.' Bastion spoke quietly. He was battling the pain, too.

'The cloak?' I asked Liyana.

'Do you think I have one lying around?' She raised an imperious eyebrow. 'It will be made and delivered to your Coven tower.'

'We need it soon.'

'It will be delivered as soon as possible,' she promised tersely. She gestured to the door in clear dismissal, and I guessed it was time to leave. We slid out of Melva's – Liyana's – office.

'Amber,' Nell called as I walked out.

I turned back. 'Yeah?'

Nell sniffed. 'I've seen salads dressed better than you. Try looking in the mirror next time.'

Try as I might, I couldn't stop the broad grin sliding onto my face as we walked out. Bastion shook his head. 'Women are strange,' he said finally. 'Why are you *happy* that she insulted your dress sense?'

Oscar started the engine. 'Because it's a return to the status quo,' he chimed in. 'Nell has always insulted Amber.'

'Exactly,' I agreed.

We were ten minutes from the Coven tower when a truck blindsided us from a side road. There was the crunch of metal and a short, sharp, scream. Mine. Luckily this time I didn't hit my head; it already hurt enough without concussion being added to it. I was still blinking in confusion when Oscar and Bastion climbed out of the car.

I followed them and my sense of déjà vu increased. Our attackers were ogres, just like they had been last time. But this time they were undead ones.

Chapter 36

The ogres' bodies were horrifyingly familiar. I'd have bet my bottom dollar that these were the same ones that had attacked us last time. Their flesh had started to decay and their clothes had a fine covering of dirt. They smelled of earth and rot and my stomach roiled.

'Ogre zombies! Oh Goddess. They're already dead! What do we do?' I shouted at Bastion in panic. I fumbled for my athame. I was not a warrior, I was just a witch.

'We kill them again!' Bastion called back. 'Permanently this time. Do you have a bomb?'

I reached into my pocket and encountered the reassuring weight of the potion vial. 'I do!'

'Keep it in reserve unless things get dicey,' he called. 'Stay out of the way and leave this to Oscar and me.'

The thing is, I'm not too good at following orders. I could definitely do *something* helpful; hanging out with

Jinx had taught me to think on my feet. I ignored the adrenaline rush, pushed away the panic and forced myself to think. Then I opened my tote bag and looked at my potions. I could work with this.

I had the bone-setting potion with me and I could tweak its use. Maybe. If not, I'd paint some runes on the ground. No harm, no foul. I pulled out a brush and painted *gengente* to provoke the opposite reaction to the potion I was using. Instead of bringing something together, I wanted to divide. Then I painted *uruz* for power or force, *dagaz* for transformation and *hagalaz* for destruction.

I stepped back from the huge runes I'd painted and pulled my magic forward. The runes lit up and the ground trembled a little at first, and then a lot more. Whoops. Maybe I'd used a little too much power; I'd intended to make a small pit to shove the ogres into, not start an earthquake.

The tremors increased in force. 'Hold on to something!' I shouted in warning to Oscar and Bastion.

'What have you done?' Oscar asked as the ground started to rumble.

I didn't bother to answer because it would soon be evident. The road rippled and trembled. A small hole appeared at first, as I'd intended, but before I could crow in triumph I noticed that it didn't stop growing. Soon it was bigger than a council-neglected pothole. The ground shuddered under our feet then tore open.

A large ravine appeared, cutting through the road and into the grass verges. The rift was as long as I could see. Rune ruin! That was a mite bigger than I'd intended. Still, a huge chasm would be useful. And although the earth had been divided, I was sure I could heal it again. Probably.

I sent a triumphant grin to Bastion. Ha! I was not just a pretty face. 'Stay out of the way' indeed!

The zombie ogres were slow to react to the gaping ravine – the undead aren't the sharpest athames in the box – but Bastion's reaction was lightning fast. He shifted into griffin form and flung himself upwards. When he was airborne, he grabbed one of the eight-foot ogres with his claws, effortlessly rose up with him in his talons then dropped him into the hole.

Oscar took a similar approach; he used the IR to shove the ogre closest to the chasm into its gaping maw. Nice.

The men quickly found their rhythm and the undead ogres found their doom. I could hear their bodies whump as they hit the bottom but such was the depth of the hole I couldn't see them. When all of the reanimated bodies had been reburied, we took a breath to evaluate the situation.

'Nice work,' Bastion commented with a half-smile. 'But you'd better fix the sinkhole before the Connection get wind of it.' Calling it a sinkhole was like calling a hurricane a breeze, but not much fazed Bastion.

'I'm on it,' I confirmed. I used the bone-setting potion again but this time I didn't use *gengente* to reverse it. I painted on a large *uruz* for power before adding a *jera* for completion and a *sowilo* for health. After a moment's hesitation, I added *dagaz* for transformation.

I was suddenly nervous. Without the threat of the ogres looming over me, I doubted the wisdom of my action. My head still hurt and I wasn't thinking as clearly as I should for this sort of thing. I couldn't afford to make a mistake.

I felt a wave of emotion from Bastion and it took me a moment to decipher it. Faith. He believed in me. It steadied me.

'Hold on,' I cautioned Oscar and Bastion, then drew my magic forward through the large runes. They lit up, the ground trembled again and we braced ourselves. For a moment I thought the rift was getting worse but then it slowly started to close. I leaned into the *sowilo* a little more, making sure the uprooted grasses found their way to the earth again unharmed by their jaunt.

'I think you've been selling yourself short,' I commented to Bastion. 'Those ogres had to weigh more than six hundred kilograms.'

'I think *you've* been selling yourself short,' he countered. 'You're a specialist in runes, potions *and* mayhem.'

'That was rather impressive, wasn't it?' I allowed myself a small smile of satisfaction.

'Very impressive. In fact, it was very sexy,' he murmured. I felt his blood heat.

A kraa interrupted our moment and Fehu plunged towards us. 'You're late,' Bastion grunted. 'You missed the party.'

The raven landed on Bastion's shoulder and hung his head. 'It's not your fault,' I reassured him. 'I used magic to end things rather quickly, otherwise you'd have been perfectly on time.'

He brightened, gave me a happy kraa, flew to my shoulder and hopped from one foot to another. If he'd had a tongue, he'd have been sticking it out at Bastion.

I felt Bastion's amusement – and that was when I realised that was all I felt. The all-pervading agony he'd been experiencing had disappeared. 'Hang on a minute! Your pain has gone!' I pointed out brightly.

He blinked. 'It has.' He had a light-bulb moment. 'The shift healed the headache.' He groaned aloud. 'I'm an idiot. I've never shifted to heal something like a headache before. Open the bond, give me the rest of the pain and I can shift again and get rid of it.'

Bastion pulled at the bond and this time I let him take all the pain. In seconds he shifted and the hurt vanished between us, like ballast being thrown from a hot-air balloon. In that moment, we were blissfully free of pain.

I couldn't help but wonder how long it would last.

Chapter 37

Bastion and I were having a cup of tea, snuggling on the sofa with my legs strewn across his lap. *The calm before the storm,* I thought cynically.

I had rung Krieg and told him about the attack. I didn't hold him responsible but he deserved to know what had happened to the bodies of his people. He had stayed on the line whilst one of his men checked the ogres' gravesite and his fury had crackled down the phone when they discovered mounds of earth and empty graves.

'This will not be borne,' he spat. 'I will destroy the necromancer that dares animate our people.'

'There's the small matter of finding them first,' I pointed out.

'I will find them and I will destroy them,' he growled. He hung up without so much as a ta-ta.

I was pleased I wasn't on his hit list any longer – I don't like having powerful enemies – but he hung up before I could suggest we work together to find the necromancer. I'd let him stew in his rage a bit then contact him another day.

My brain felt clear and focused. I gave a happy hum. 'It's so nice being pain free,' I said.

A surge of guilt and embarrassment hit me. 'I'm sorry,' Bastion said quietly. 'I don't know why it didn't occur to me sooner to shift. I've never used the shift to heal something other than a gaping stab wound.' He cleared his throat awkwardly. 'I'm pretty embarrassed.' He was downplaying it; he was completely mortified.

'It doesn't matter,' I said lightly. 'We'll know for next time.'

He raised my socked foot and kissed it, making me laugh. 'Thank you for your forgiveness, Bambi.'

'You don't need it.' I brushed it away. 'You did nothing wrong.'

'I left you in agony!' The words burst from him in self-directed fury.

'You took half of it! Enough, Bastion, I have no interest in seeing you self-flagellate.' I paused. 'Unless that's something that gets your rocks off. I'll never yuck your yum,' I promised.

Bastion grinned. 'No, that's not one of my kinks.'

'Good to know.' I realised that might sound judge-mental, as if I were glad that wasn't one of his kinks, and that was not what I had intended. I forced myself to continue instead, 'But I'm really up for trying anything at least once if you like it.' My cheeks reddened. 'I don't want our sex life to be focused solely on *my* fantasies.'

Before Bastion, it had been years since I'd had sex. I was well aware, even in the few orgasmic days that we'd spent together, that I was still pretty inexperienced compared to him. I was keen to remedy that. More importantly, this chat about kinks had thoroughly dis-tracted him from feeling bad about the whole headache debacle.

'You're my fantasy,' he growled, pulling me in for a hard, possessive kiss that made my head spin. Parts of my body tingled at his attention and I groaned aloud. Things might have gotten very interesting if someone hadn't knocked at the door at that precise moment.

We slid apart as Oscar stalked in carrying a large cardboard box. He threw it down onto the coffee table dramatically. 'Your cloak,' he proclaimed to Bastion.

Bastion leaned forward, opened the lid and carefully pulled out the cloak. He stood and effortlessly whirled it around his shoulders, looking for all the world as if he put it on every day.

He raised the hood and his face disappeared – even his eyes vanished from sight. You could tell from the fall of the cloak that he was large and bulky, and most people who saw him would assume he was male. Not much could be done about that, but otherwise he was wholly incognito. Even his clothes had disappeared from view in a swirl of atmospheric black smoke. The Seers are so dramatic.

My phone blared: Voltaire. I swiped to answer and hit speakerphone so we could all hear him. 'DeLea,' I announced.

As usual, he dispensed with pleasantries. 'We have a problem.'

Didn't we always? 'What?' I asked brusquely.

'The auction is taking place in Edinburgh.' He paused. 'In two hours.'

I was close to letting an expletive slip out. That was all-but asking the impossible, unless the vampyrs wanted to help get us there by phasing us through the shadows, and frankly I'd rather have stroked a lizard than trust Voltaire to transport us. 'Where?' I asked.

'Chimera Auction House, Frampton Place.'

'We'll be there.' Probably. I hung up. 'Griffin Air?' I asked Bastion.

'We've no choice,' he agreed grimly. 'We can't wait for a helicopter, there's no time. Even with my best efforts, two hours is going to be an ask.'

'I believe in you.' I smiled because I did. 'Let's go.'

Oscar huffed. 'He won't be able to carry us both.'

'No,' Bastion agreed as he disappeared into the bedroom to fetch his harness from his bag. It belatedly occurred to me that I should give him a drawer or something so he wasn't living out of his duffel bag, but the thought scared the life out of me. I wasn't seriously thinking of asking him to move in formally, right? Was a drawer moving in? He was bonded forever to me as my familiar, but for some reason clearing out a drawer for him felt like a big deal.

Too soon. I tabled the drawer issue; I had no time to think about that now.

Bastion came back in carrying his black backpack and the harness. 'We have to go. You'll have to keep an eye on things here,' he directed Oscar.

'Where are you going?' A voice popped up. 'I'll come.'

'Frogmatch!' I clutched my hand to my heart. 'You scared the heck out of me.'

'Sorry, Ellie.' The imp grinned widely, not repentant in the slightest.

I gave him a side-eyed glance. Surely Bastion would have been aware of the imp's presence if he'd been there during our make-out session… 'We're going to Scotland, to a black-magic auction.'

'Cool! I'll come.'

I pressed my lips together, reluctant to endanger him. He read my face and his jocular expression faded. 'They cut off my tail, Ellie. I deserve to be part of this as much as you do. Don't think that because I'm small, I don't get rights.'

'Of course you do!' I said instantly.

'Good, then I'm coming.' He scurried up the table leg onto the table and then clambered up me like I was a climbing frame before settling on my shoulder. I wanted to quiz Frogmatch about what he'd learned whilst he was spying on the Coven, but we didn't have time to get into an in-depth conversation. We were fighting against the clock. Surely if he'd found out anything important, he'd have mentioned it.

I focused on the immediate task: getting us to Scotland. 'Do you have both cloaks in the backpack?' I asked Bastion. We'd be in real trouble if we went all that way and then couldn't obscure our identities.

'I do,' he assured me.

I hastily packed a few potions in my tote, then we strode up to the Coven tower roof. Bastion shimmered into griffin form. I laid the harness down for him to step into and secured it around him. His backpack had vanished with his shift but, like his clothing, it would return when he changed back to human. I wondered where the heck it went – but magic has very little to do with logic.

As I climbed on top of Bastion I frowned at Frogmatch, who was still resting on my shoulder. He couldn't stay there at the speed we'd be flying at. 'Don't make this weird,' I instructed him, 'but you'd better climb into my blouse. We can't have you falling from these heights.'

Face solemn, he didn't make any titty jokes just held up his hands. I deposited him in the V of my bra, facing him outwards so he could peek over the lace. I secured goggles over my eyes, laced my fingers through the leather strap and squeezed Bastion with my legs to signal that I was ready.

I needed to make a couple of calls but we were in a hurry; they would have to wait until we were underway. Was there a phone signal at 5,000 feet?

Taking my breath away, Bastion bolted forward and leapt off the edge of the building. My heart caught in my throat – then his wings snapped out and we soared. It was his joy that got me. It was vibrant and pure, and it sang to me down our bond, infectious in its simplicity.

Even as the air whipped around me and we flew towards evil, I found I was smiling.

Chapter 38

Bastion got us to Edinburgh in less than two hours, probably breaking some sort of griffin record. When he shifted back to human he looked even bulkier, as if the workout in griffin form had strengthened his human one.

'Frogmatch!' I said, suddenly panicking. 'Have you killed someone recently? There are wards and only those that have just killed can come in. You'll have to stay outside.' Dammit, why had I forgotten that?

Frogmatch blinked at me before nodding reluctantly. 'Yes, I've killed recently.'

I gaped. He'd killed someone? How? A car wreck, perhaps? Imps did so love to sabotage cars, trains and planes. Something about metal really seemed to piss them off.

Bastion seemed unsurprised. He always treated the imp with a sort of wary respect that seemed at odds with Frogmatch's diminutive size.

'We'll be fine then,' I said briskly, like my view of him hadn't changed. I liked the imp – as much as I liked anyone – but if he was responsible for some innocent human dying...? I needed to know more before I judged him unfairly, but now wasn't the time or place. Still, it reminded me that I really didn't know much about my indentured imp.

Bastion and I settled our cloaks around us, concealing our clothes and faces in shadow. 'The cowls are great. It's so handy that you don't have to wear makeup,' I noted.

'Yes,' Bastion agreed, deadpan. 'It saved me hours of getting-ready time.'

I snorted with laughter and some of my tension eased. Sure, we were sneaking into an invite-only black auction, but I was with Bastion so it would be fine. He probably did this sort of thing all of the time. This was a walk in the park for him.

'That's better,' he murmured. 'Remember, we belong here. We're here to look around and gather information and – if the opportunity arises – to buy a really evil jewel. Nothing more.'

'I'm not good at this cloak-and-dagger stuff,' I admitted.

I couldn't see his face but I felt his amusement and I didn't doubt that he was grinning at me. He reached under my cloak to touch my athame – my dagger – which was resting in an ankle holster, then tugged at my cloak. 'I'd say you're pretty good at this cloak-and-dagger stuff.'

I gave him a flat look that was spoiled by him not being able to see it. 'Funny guy. Just hilarious.' I cleared my throat. 'Let's go.'

He nodded. Humour was replaced with determination and alertness; he was ready for danger. That made one of us.

Frogmatch concealed himself again inside my top and we walked towards the entrance of the Chimera Auction House. It was getting dark but the streets were bustling, so nobody paid us any attention. No doubt the Common realmers simply thought we were doing cosplay and we'd used make-up to conceal our faces. The Other realm's magic goes to quite some lengths to persuade Common realmers that they never see anything amiss.

The auction house was well lit. It was a grand old building that had recently been gutted and renovated. There was no queue outside, though I saw a number of ogres acting as security: hired hands. Fury rocketed through me. Each species has rogues but to my knowledge, ogres are the exception to that rule. Rogue ogres are hunted down and killed; if you aren't part of the den, you are dead to them. Literally.

Krieg's men were here, so he *knew* about this gathering of black witches yet he'd said nothing. The bastard! I'd spoken to him on the phone earlier and, despite his fury with the black witches and the necromantic witch who'd possessed his men, he'd still said nothing!

'Easy, Bambi,' Bastion murmured, feeling my rage. 'We need to keep a level head.'

I realised my anger was affecting him as I felt his temper bubbling, growing, being swept along by mine. I took a deep breath and forced myself to settle down. There would be time for recriminations later.

'Okay,' I said tightly. 'I'm calm.' Jinx's lie detector would have pinged if she'd heard me say that, but I was definitely calm*er*, though rage was simmering beneath the surface in a wrathful torrent that I tried to ignore. Damn Krieg! Could I trust no one in this forsaken realm?

We approached the imposing entrance to the building. Someone had laid down a red carpet and as soon as I stepped on it I knew that they had painted a tonne of truth runes under it. Rune ruin! That made things a helluva lot trickier.

No doubt Bastion sensed the same. 'Let me take lead,' he murmured. I said nothing; he'd take my silence as acquiescence.

We approached the ogres. Next to them was a petite woman, gaunt and pale as if she hadn't seen the sun in a while. She looked starved and sick. 'They are both full of rage,' she murmured to the hulking ogre beside her.

'And?' the ogre said.

'I sense three living beings and a familiar bond.'

'I have my familiar with me,' Bastion said coolly, implying that the third living being was his familiar.

'What is your purpose in coming here?' the ogre asked.

'I intend to pay an exorbitant amount of money for the harkan crystal,' Bastion responded.

'True,' the lady murmured. Was she an empath relying on the truth runes we stood upon, or a truth-seeker like Jinx? I hadn't heard of another one in at least a generation. I studied her with interest. She looked like a firm breeze would push her over.

'Obviously,' the ogre snorted. 'He's standing on enough runes to force Nixon to tell the truth.' In a less dire situation, I would have laughed. 'Have you killed someone recently?' he asked.

'Of course,' Bastion said smoothly.

'And you?' The ogre pointed to me.

'Yes,' I said simply.

'Do you have any phones on you?'

'No,' Bastion declared.

'No,' I confirmed. Bastion had warned me that it was unlikely we'd be able to take phones or weapons inside, so my tote bag, potions, athame and our phones were tucked behind a bin a few streets away. I hoped they'd still be there when we got back. Bastion still had his backpack in his hands, which looked somewhat incongruous with the cloak.

The ogre patted us down impersonally and we walked through the metal detectors. He rooted around in Bastion's bag then looked impressed. I should have looked to see what was inside it; it couldn't be weapons because he handed it back to Bastion without further comment.

I heard steps behind us and turned. Another cloak wearer was waiting patiently. Huh. How many of these bespelled cloaks did the Seers make?

The ogre waved us in. 'What is your purpose in coming here?' he started asking the next entrant.

We swept inside.

Chapter 39

The room was depressingly large, as was the number of its occupants. I stared around in dismay, though thankfully the cowl hid my reaction. There were so many witches here. How could so many have followed a path of evil?

I heard some words in French and then some German. Relief sank in as I realised this wasn't just the UK's black witches but evidently some of Europe's, too. It appeared that the black Coven was a worldwide outfit. Brilliant.

I tried not to let my apprehension slide across my bond to Bastion. We were in a room full of people who killed for power and they weren't going to let a spying white witch walk away; if we were discovered, it would be curtains for me. I tried to shove down my apprehension. Didn't the prophecy say that the black witches would tremble at me? At the moment it felt like the other way around.

Everyone was in disguise and, almost without exception, they were using Seer-bespelled cloaks. How much were the Seers making out of the black witches? That was certainly a line I could tug; if I could get names of who purchased them, I'd have one heck of a suspect list. I wasn't sure if Liyana would share that information, though she'd seemed to warm a little to me by the end of our meeting. If she refused, the only way to get that list would be through the Connection and I was loathe to involve the Inspectors.

There was a tangible aura in the room. Power and darkness crackled in every recess and alcove of the building. Everyone here used blood, torture and death to augment their magic. There were obvious cliques, too: huddles of four witches here or five witches there.

Bastion and I stood out like a sore thumb as the only twosome. Witches, even black witches, need to be a part of a Coven. Heads twisted towards us and, although I couldn't see the suspicious glares hidden under the cloaks, I was certain they were there.

I threaded my arm through Bastion's and deliberately moved us a little closer to another group under the guise of examining the room's centrepiece. It helped us blend in a little more. I hoped.

The sumptuous room had polished teak floors. Teak is hardwearing and I dreaded to think what use these floors had seen. Black columns rose floor to ceiling and the walls were freshly painted a soft cream that complemented the red carpets on various raised daises. Chairs had been set out, and in the centre of the room there was a vase on a pedestal holding an opulent floral display.

The items that were up for sale weren't on display. There was no catalogue to browse through, so I guessed they were planning a big dramatic reveal. Waiters and waitresses circulated offering sparkling wine and I looked at it longingly. I took one in order to fit in, but I didn't dare sip it. The last thing I needed was to consume some sort of hidden potion or poison. My entanglement – and poisoning – with Becky was fresh in my mind.

'Thank goodness for that,' Frogmatch piped up. 'I was nervous that killing that fly last week wouldn't count as me properly killing someone.'

'You killed a *fly?*' I was aghast. We'd risked his life by bringing him, believing that he'd recently killed. There I was, imagining Frogmatch sabotaging cars and buses and killing innocent humans, and this whole time his crime had been to kill a fly.

'It was a really big one,' he said defensively. 'And it wouldn't get out when I opened the window.'

I couldn't see Bastion's face but I knew he was grinning. 'You could have *died!*' I hissed.

'We'll discuss it later,' Bastion interrupted. 'Eyes on the prize, everyone.' His gentle rebuke was enough to calm me. He was right: now wasn't the time, but we would examine Frogmatch's foolhardy attitude later. I was going to write him a full report about all the things he'd done wrong, but for now I shelved it. We didn't need to draw any more unwanted attention.

Bastion and I waited patiently for the auction to begin as our wine slowly warmed in our hands. The murmur of voices around us was infuriating because it was next to impossible for me to differentiate the voices to get any useful intel. I hoped Bastion, with his super hearing, was having better luck.

Finally someone in a sharp pinstripe suit banged a gavel. He wore no cloak, and clearly worked for the auction house. The room was galvanised into action and there was an audible buzz as everyone moved towards the chairs. Bastion and I picked two chairs at the end of the aisle, close to the walls and escape – if we needed it. It's not paranoia when they really are out to get you.

The man in the suit stepped aside, giving the gavel to a cowl-covered witch. Thank goodness we had accidentally complied with the dress code, though in truth it wasn't really luck because witches have used bespelled cloaks for centuries. It's our go-to disguise; how wonderfully predictable we are.

From what Ria had told me, the black Coven operated in cells. No one knew more than a handful of other black witches so that they couldn't betray anyone else if they were caught. Consequently a meeting like this required anonymity for everyone present.

The witch who now held the gavel spoke in a thick French accent. His deep voice echoed around the room. 'It is wonderful to see so many of you could join us at such short notice. I am grateful to our family that have travelled so far to be with us today. I know there have been grave concerns about our familiars' continuing ill health.'

A loud murmur passed through the crowd.

'To that end, the potion work of Madame X has continued to be resourceful and proactive.' His voice darkened. 'But as yet, she has not been able to *solve* the problem. However, she has given temporary energy to our familiars so that we can remain undetected within our so-called Covens. Samples of her enlivening potion will be handed out as you leave the auction tonight. Those samples are free. If you require more, do make further enquiries. In the same vein, the forcible removal of tails continues to provide the best pain treatment. The agony of such an act certainly continues to sustain us and our familiars for an extended period.'

Hidden in my top, Frogmatch let out an enraged growl. I coughed to hide the sound, not daring to look around to see if anyone was looking at me oddly. The tails! I had thought it was just a crazy vampyr on the loose but suddenly everything was clear. Even the tail of poor Cindy, Ria's familiar, had been removed. I had thought it a brutal, horrific message, a warning to the member of my Coven, but now it took on a more sinister aspect. I didn't just have a few stray vampyrs to worry about because they were just hired hands – either willingly or unwillingly.

The necromancer who'd killed Melva through a possessed vampyr was certainly busy. My stomach lurched; what if there was more than one necromancer? After all, Hilary had been one as well. How many of these black witches around me were necromancers who could re-animate the dead and possess vampyrs?

I wondered if the bastard that had killed Melva was here. My fists clenched and it took everything in me to sit still and look at the Frenchman who was still pontificating.

'I will now pass you into the capable hands of Mr Mc-Goughlin, our auctioneer. The opening lot will be a box of specially curated tails. I can verify the taste of agony on this bunch is truly delectable.' There were polite claps, like all of this was *normal.* I thought I might be sick.

McGoughlin, in his sharp pinstripe suit, stepped back up to the microphone. He took the gavel from French Guy. 'Opening bid for the Box o' Tails is £500.' The bidding increased rapidly until the small box finally went for just shy of £13,000, when McGoughlin finally let the gavel fall. Frogmatch was bubbling with fury, his skin getting progressively hotter as his anger rose. I was sure I could detect the faint smell of brimstone.

Next up was a brooch that would ensure the wearer passed out within thirty minutes of having it pinned on. After the brooch, things went from sinister to nightmarish very quickly. The lamenting mirror, or mirror of tears, caused madness in anyone that gazed in it for twenty minutes. The truly dark thing about it was that it wasn't twenty minutes in one go but a cumulative effect. If you wanted to drive your enemy mad, all you needed do was gift them this mirror and be patient; eventually the quick glances would add up, even if they weren't vain enough to stare at themselves. The mirror went for an horrific £100,000. It seemed that the witches gathered here were eager to turn their enemies mad. I shivered.

The shadow skull went next for an eye-watering £250,000. It was sentient and stored the memories of both its original owner and the dozens of subsequent ones that had bonded with it. There were apparently a plethora of dark spells locked inside it. It reminded me uncomfortably of Grimmy.

Each item shocked me with its vileness. There was a cursed harp, a necro dagger and an ancient grimoire made of human skin. A number of items focused on removing people's free will, forcing them into subservience or some semblance of cursed love. It was appalling how high the bidding went for those items.

But it was the last item that we'd all come to see.

The cloaked witch with the French accent brought it in. A gong sounded pretentiously and we all watched as he carried in a glass box containing a dark-red crystal. He walked through the assembly at a slow march, as if it were a wedding and he was the bride. This was the crown jewel of the auction; it was for *this* that people had travelled across oceans. A harkan crystal, a real one too.

The room vibrated with a power that was so strong it made my teeth ache. The implication of its size made my heart weep. So many had died for this piece of vile magic to come into being, hundreds – even thousands. It surprised me that it was for sale. I would have thought that the black witch owner would cling to it with all their might.

The room bubbled with excitement; whispers broke out and people were leaning forward in their seats. Next to me Bastion did the same, and I shifted forward too. As I moved, Frogmatch took advantage of the swirl of my cloak to sidle out of my top, down one of the cloak's folds and run away. Rune ruin! Where was that damned imp going?

I dared not shout after him. I'd felt his anger at the Box o' Tails and all that had followed. His skin had become progressively hotter against mine until I'd been sure he must be burning me with his rage. I had no idea what he was thinking or planning, but it couldn't be good.

My stomach twisted in fear for him, and I silently prayed for the Goddess to watch over him.

Chapter 40

I struggled to pretend I was interested in the harkan crystal when all I wanted to do was to look around for Frogmatch. I only refocused on the stage because I had to. French Guy had finally reached the podium, having completed his stately march.

'Here is what you have all come for,' he intoned. 'The Harkan Crystal of Delilah. A work of centuries in the making, it has come before you for sale only at the Leader's insistence.'

The name Delilah felt important and somehow sounded familiar but I couldn't place it other than hearing it being crooned by Tom Jones.

'The Leader should have the crystal!' Someone shouted from the back.

'He can use it to break the Coven Council in two!' someone else called. I wondered if they were plants, placed by the Leader to initiate those thoughts.

'Is he here?' an eager feminine voice called.

French Guy laughed. 'But of course he is here, *mes amis*. He would not miss this for all the world. Now, let us commence bidding at one million pounds.'

There was a hush before someone bid. To my surprise, Bastion counter-bid. I struggled to keep the shock off my face, then I realised that with the cowl up I really didn't have to.

A third player entered the bidding but Bastion showed no signs of letting up. Finally the third player dropped out, leaving only Bastion and the initial bidder in the running. Tension ran through me as my griffin bid more and more.

He had no authority to bid from the Coven Council; every penny he was bidding was his own hard-earned cash. I hoped he had a plan for recouping it or the guilt of bringing him here would cripple me. I should have known he couldn't lie under truth runes; he really had been planning on spending an exorbitant amount of money to secure the harkan crystal.

Things seemed to be getting heated until the other man abruptly lowered his paddle and didn't raise it again. The last bid standing was Bastion's.

'Going once,' French Guy said.

The initial bidder sat down and I battled disbelief. Were we really going to do it, secure the harkan crystal away from the black witches? My heart was pounding. It couldn't be this easy, could it? Triumph was so close, I could almost taste it. Victory pie would do nicely.

'Going twice,' French Guy said, drawing out the tension.

Everyone around the initial bidder turned to him in surprise. I couldn't see their faces but their reaction suggested shock and maybe even a little aggression. I'd bet my bottom dollar that Bastion was using his coaxing skills on the other buyers and that was why they'd dropped out. That was why their companions were so surprised at their about-turn.

'Sold!' The gavel swung down. 'To the man on the seventh row.'

Someone walked up to French Guy and whispered in his ear. He was hooked up to the sound system so we all heard when the Frenchman started swearing viciously. He cut himself off with effort.

'It seems, *mes amis*, that we have *un petit* security issue. The vampyrs have phased in and opened the way to the Connection's little Inspectors. We will be discussing this with the witch responsible for runing the hall.' His voice was hard, threatening violence.

A witch stood up at the back of the hall, downed a potion and keeled over. She gave some choked gurgles as she clutched her throat that was hidden under the shadows of her cloak. In the silence that had fallen, we all heard her last shuddering breath.

She fell to the floor, dead. French Guy gave a satisfied nod. '*Bon*. Now, it is time for a quick getaway.' He turned to Bastion and called out in a voice full of faux regret, 'Sorry, sir, it looks like we'll be keeping the harkan after all.'

His hands emerged from his cloak and he snapped on some gloves. When he wore adequate protection, he opened the box, reached into it and drew out the red crystal. He handed it reverently to the cloaked man standing next to him.

This man, whom I assumed was the Leader, took the crystal in his gloved hands. The red crystal pulsed and he seemed to be wrestling with it somehow. With a huge grunt of effort, he managed to use the sharp point of the harkan crystal to cut his forearm. The red blood welled and ran down his pale-skinned arm. He'd cut deeply, I suspected more deeply than he'd intended because of the crystal's lack of acquiescence.

He dipped his gloved finger into his blood and painted it in the air. I had never seen anything like it – the rune hung like it had been painted on parchment. The crystal glowed with a malevolent red light and as it pulsed, five cloaked figures fell to the floor. They were unmoving, and I suspected, dead. Using the harkan came at a steep price. The malicious jewel pulsed again and a portal was ripped into existence. It grew, flickering with flames and evil intent.

I peered through it and recognised the two castles on the other side and the flying beasts behind them. My mouth dropped open. The daemon realm: he'd opened a portal to the daemon realm with *one* rune, a tonne of power and five deaths. It shouldn't have been possible, but then he'd painted a rune on *air*. I was going to have to re-evaluate what was possible and what was not. The knowledge he must have...

'Quickly!' French Guy said to the assemblage. 'Through here. We will use the return gate to get back to the Other realm.' Without hesitation, the cloaked figures poured towards the daemon gate. And that was when the door behind us flew open.

'Everyone freeze!' Inspector Elvira of the Connection barked. When no one obeyed her, the IR came into play. The Connection's wizards used it to hold and seize the nearest witches but the witches outnumbered them and not everyone was fleeing. I watched, sickened, as a black cloud literally tore a detective apart as he screamed. I looked around desperately for a flash of red but, try as I might, I couldn't see hide nor hair of Frogmatch.

A breath on my ear made ice slide down my spine then a voice next to me murmured, 'Time to make a swift exit, my daughter.' The tone was warm, affectionate.

Everything in me froze as I recognised it from my re-claimed memories of my father. This time it wasn't dis-torted by a vampyr's possession, it was *his* voice. I whirled around but there was only Bastion by my side. How was my father speaking to me? Was it some sort of audio-astral projection?

'The Connection won't differentiate between black and white witches when you're wearing the cowl,' my father continued casually. 'They'll use deadly force.' He spoke to Bastion. 'You have a plan to get her out of here, griffin?'

'I have my own plan!' I interrupted hotly.

A soft laugh. 'No doubt, Amber. Then use it. Now!'

Much as I hated to obey him, he was right. 'The walls!' I called to Bastion.

As we started towards the cream walls, a roar rang out and the whole room shook with the force of it. In the far corner, where black witches were fighting the Connection, a small red figure was starting to grow. The witches around him were shouting frantically, grabbing crystals from their pockets, throwing them around the imp, trying to contain him.

'Frogmatch!' I screamed. 'Run!'

Focused on growing, he paid me no heed. He grew until he was the same size as me and then he kept going. His antlers, cute when tiny, were deadly in full size. He bent his head and rammed them into the nearest black witches. They screamed as he eviscerated them. Then his claws came into play, lashing out and neatly disembowelling the nearest witch.

'Leader, get the imp!' one of the witches screamed. A beat later, the red of the harkan crystal crackled out. As it did so, the one who had called out for help also fell to the jewel's deadly power. A harkan was fuelled by death, but something was stopping the black witches from accessing its power without deadly consequences. Thank the Goddess for small mercies. The red pulse from the jewel struck Frogmatch in the heart and in an instant he was pint sized again. Frogmatch fell to the floor, unmoving.

Bastion dragged me towards the walls. 'We have to help him!' I yelled.

'He's too far away,' Bastion said grimly. 'We have to get you to safety. We'll come back for him,' he promised.

The crystals around Frogmatch lit up as he was forcibly contained by the black witches and shoved into a crate. Dammit, Bastion was right. The whole thing was utter chaos: the black witches were fighting tooth and claw, and the Connection were using deadly force back at them. If we tried to save Frogmatch now, we'd be killed in the mêlée.

We bolted for the walls. Skidding to a stop in front of all of that magnolia, my heart hammered as I reached out and touched it. Benji had to be here. He had to be! But the walls stayed cool and flat.

I turned to face the approaching Inspectors, my mind blank. I had no plan. I couldn't use my potion bomb on them; they didn't deserve death because they were just doing their job.

I was so screwed.

Chapter 41

Before I could descend into total panic, familiar hands grabbed me around my waist. I had a moment to take a deep breath and then Benji pulled me into the walls. The walls were thin; when I'd set up this plan, I had envisaged that he would simply pop me through this wall and into another corridor from which I could make my escape.

But he did not. After he dragged me into the wall, I lost all sense of where we were or how we were moving. My chest was straining and I was dying to take a breath, even though it would be full of brick and dust and would almost certainly kill me. I held my breath and strained not to give in to the urge just to breathe.

Thank the Goddess, just when I thought I was going to pass out, we burst from the walls. I gratefully choked down gulps of air, my lungs screaming at me for my idiocy.

'Crikey, Benji,' I said when I'd recovered a little. 'Warn a lady before you do that to her!'

'I'm sorry, Am Bam,' he whispered contritely, 'but there was no time. The Coven Council knows about the Connection raid and they are trying to catalogue the whereabouts of every witch in the city. If anyone appears to be missing, they will be added to a master list of black-witch suspects. I couldn't have you on that list. All over the UK, all of the Coven bodyguards are undertaking Coven-wide sweeps. They'll be here any second.'

It was gratifying that the lumbering Coven Council appeared to be making some fast moves for once. I wondered how much Kass had had to yell to get them moving.

Bastion stepped out of the walls with the other golem, David. Unlike me, Bastion simply took in a shallow breath like his lungs weren't on fire. Show off.

'Cloaks, quickly!' Benji said urgently.

We both whipped them off and threw them at him. He balled them up and shoved them into the wall. 'That's a handy storage space,' I remarked drily. A small corner of the cloak poked out of the wall and David pushed it until it disappeared.

'Sit!' Benji said urgently, his eyes glowing white as he tapped into some magic of his own that I didn't understand. He blinked and his eyes cleared.

I looked around. We appeared to be in a bedsit, sitting at a dining-room table. It was dimly lit with only one naked bulb hanging from the ceiling. Industrial chic.

The walls had posters of Nirvana and Red Hot Chilli Peppers, which made me smile. I knew then without a doubt that we were in Benji's room; he had taken to rock music like a selkie to water.

The single bed in the corner was neatly made, but I grimaced at the thought that the only room Benji had was a lousy underground bedsit. I vowed to improve his living conditions. He might have returned for David, but that didn't mean he had to live in a hovel. It reminded me uncomfortably of the jail cell Mack had shoved me into.

The door burst open and, as if summoned by my thoughts, none other than Mack, walked in. When he saw me, he let out a growl. 'Dammit! I don't care if you're here. I *know* you're evil.'

I stared at him like I had no idea what he was talking about. 'Did you get hit on the head?' I asked, exasperated. I looked at the men behind him. 'He should see a medical professional.'

'There has been a raid on a black Coven,' one of the men behind Mack said. 'Any missing witches are suspect. We're here to get the golems to help in the search.'

'Then what in the Goddess's name are you waiting for? Go! Search the whole damned catacombs as fast as you can! You're wasting time – they'll be able to get back through. You have to hurry!' My urgency broke through and everyone whirled out, including Benji and David.

At the exit, Mack paused. 'Just because you're here doesn't exempt you. You just missed this meeting for whatever reason. I *know* you're evil.'

'So you keep saying,' I sighed. 'But frankly, of the two of us I *know* who is evil and it isn't me. The worst thing of all is that you don't know that you are.'

Bad people make bad choices all over the world and have no idea that they are the villains in the story. They have their own narratives to justify their heinous actions, as no doubt Mack did.

With one last glower, he left.

Chapter 42

Benji and David returned soon afterwards. I had spent the intervening period wringing my hands and envisaging horrific things happening to Frogmatch. I shouldn't have let the little – large? – guy come along for the ride. Why had I done that? I prayed with all my might that he was fine and he'd escaped from the witches. I hoped he'd pop up any second now but, no matter how hard I looked around, I didn't see a flash of red skin and a cheeky grin. My stomach clenched.

Bastion laid his hand on mine, sending soothing vibes down our bond. I shook them off and glared at him. I didn't want to be soothed; in my fear for Frogmatch, I was as prickly as a hedgehog. I was at least partially responsible for him and I'd failed him. We'd left him, and now he was who knew where.

I tried to reign in my agitation when the two golems returned. I was pleased to see that Benji and David had become friends and Benji was clearly showing David the ropes. Usually there was only one golem awake at once. The Council didn't need to have more because, despite the bed in his room, Benji didn't need to sleep. He liked lying down, though, and pretending.

'I'll make us all some tea,' Benji said as he lumbered in. He froze. 'I'm sorry, Am, that was insensitive of me, wasn't it? After the poisoning...' He trailed off uncomfortably.

I smiled. 'I'm okay, and truthfully I need a cup of tea.' Boy, did I? I'd just lost Frogmatch and met my father, albeit in some sort of projection. He'd spoken to me in his real voice. He *knew* me, knew about Bastion. And yet he was just a shard of memory to me.

He'd known we were there the whole time, yet he hadn't given us up to the other black witches. But he'd also made me kill a vampyr. It was all so mixed up that I no longer knew which way was up.

Benji brought over my tea, placed the china cup on the table and studied me. 'Do you need a hug, friend?'

I automatically started to say no but then I nodded. I let myself be drawn against his hard, cold body. He held me for so long that his cold started to leach into my limbs, but the depths of his coldness didn't alleviate the warmth of the comfort that he brought to me.

Finally I sighed. 'Thanks Benji.' I gave him a quick kiss on the cheek and stepped back.

David's mouth was open. 'You really *are* friends.'

'We are,' I agreed, a small smile tugging at my lips.

'I am glad we saved you,' David said abruptly, giving a nod as if he were talking to himself. 'Even if we get in trouble. It is right to save a friend, I think.'

'It is,' Benji said firmly. 'It is a tenet of friendship to do so. I will save *you*, if ever you need it.'

'Thank you,' David murmured. 'That would be nice.'

I tried to smile despite the worry churning in my gut. I was happy for Benji to have someone other than me and Bastion. Benji and I were often so far apart that it made me feel better to know Benji had someone close by he could turn to.

I picked up my tea and paused as I read the mug. My very obviously brand-new mug said: *Hold on while I over-think this.* I looked over at Bastion's mug, which simply read: *Fuckoffee.* I snorted with slightly hysterical laughter. 'You got yourself some mugs!'

Benji nodded seriously. 'I am told that a hobby is a good thing. I tried golf but the ball went too far.'

David snorted quietly. 'And through a wall.'

Benji slid him a playful glare. 'The wall got in the ball's way. I tried reading, but I'm not too keen on romance. I read a sports' romance book but I am not sure what was described was anatomically possible.' He frowned. 'I even drew a diagram but I couldn't get it to work.'

Another laugh bubbled up, which I suppressed with effort – I didn't want him to think I was laughing at him. 'Maybe another type of book then – a thriller, perhaps, or a good mystery?'

He considered. 'Perhaps I will try another type of book,' he said.

'Do. Reading is one of life's greatest pleasures. A reader gets to go on a thousand adventures. You just need to find the book for you. I truly believe reading is for everyone. You could even try—' I gave a fake shudder '—non-fiction.'

'If it is important to you, I will try and find another book to read. In the meantime, I settled on collecting mugs like you. I hope you don't mind if we gather the same things. Coins and stamps did not appeal to me.'

'I'm honoured. And I can see you've been taking your rock education seriously, too.' I nodded at the posters on the wall.

'I have. I am a real head banger.' Benji spoke the words slowly, using the unfamiliar term cautiously like he wasn't sure if he was using them properly. I gave him an encouraging nod.

'Anyway,' he went on soberly, 'we should talk about the witches' searches. We've been ordered not to talk about the particulars of the list.' He sounded unhappy. Bound to the Council as he was, he couldn't circumvent the order. 'But there were quite a few people missing from each Coven. I'm sure some of them will have an explanation.'

I laughed sardonically. '*All* of them will have an explanation and some of them will even be true.' I frowned. 'I need that list, or at the very least the list for my Coven.' I rubbed my eyes. 'This is a mess. There were so many witches gathered in that room.'

'A hundred and fifty at least,' Bastion agreed. 'But they came from across Europe, perhaps the whole world. It isn't as grim as you think.'

'If they're so strong in numbers, why haven't they made some sort of move?' I asked.

'They don't seem to want the spotlight yet. They're content to pull strings,' Bastion suggested.

'They weren't ever going to sell the harkan crystal tonight, not when it can open portals like that. The power roiling off it hurt my teeth. The witches could level cities with it – so why haven't they?'

'They were wearing gloves when they handled it,' Bastion noted. 'It didn't look like it was easy to manipulate, and it killed the witches around it to use it. Maybe they haven't cracked its use yet.'

'Great, so we're on a countdown. Get the crystal off them before they work out how to use it to its full potential.'

'It seems likely.'

'Half its potential was still pretty terrifying,' I muttered. 'They opened a portal to the daemon realm and pottered through like it was a trip to shops.'

'Maybe it is for them,' Bastion said morosely. 'They're getting all those dark artefacts from somewhere.'

'Or they're making them,' I countered. 'We need that list.' Because someone on that list had Frogmatch. 'We need the list,' I repeated firmly. 'And I know just who we can talk to to get it.'

Chapter 43

Kass huffed; the huff sounded loud and grumpy over the speakerphone. 'I really can't give that to you, Amber,' she said firmly.

I'd called her because I wasn't sure whether she was back in her home Coven of Liverpool or still in Edinburgh. Apparently, she was in Edinburgh.

'I need the list,' I insisted. 'We both know that I'll only use it for good. I'm sure the Coven Council will be disseminating it to the other Coven mothers before long. We have to know who needs to be looked at more closely.'

'That is not the current plan,' she said drily. 'We don't want to blinker anyone. We all need to look internally at everyone, not just the ones noted as absent. We can't guarantee that those who are missing *are* black witches, and the Council is afraid we'll start a witch hunt.'

I should have known that the Council's decisive action was too good to be true; they were great at information gathering but glacial at action. I shook my head angrily. 'The Council is being played – a black witch is there, telling you a bunch of lies. Who said we shouldn't be looking hard at the missing witches?'

Kass's voice tightened. 'I cannot share Council's deliberations with you, Amber. You know that.'

I hissed with exasperation. 'Kass, you have got to *think*. We need this list!'

'The list is going to be given to someone else,' she blurted.

'Who?'

She paused for a long moment and I thought she wasn't going to answer. 'The Crone.'

I stilled. 'We don't have a Crone.'

She dropped her voice. 'Willow is going to be the conduit. She is starting the ceremony now. She's going to call on the Goddess to show us the identity of the new Crone.'

I blinked. 'I thought there was an application process and a test?'

'In calmer times, maybe. But the Council felt that we are in such dire straits that something needed to be done now. Willow, the Mother and the Maiden have sequestered themselves; they've already prepared the pentagram with runes. In a moment, they'll be joining us and we will see what guidance the Goddess gives us.'

Her tone was joyful and exultant. Having the Goddess channelled in your presence was a once-in-a-lifetime event. It would leave Willow exhausted for weeks, but the Council wasn't wrong: the situation was dire.

'Shouldn't it be you doing all this rather than Willow?' I asked. Whilst Kass was technically the newest member of the Council, she was also its most senior one. She was the Coven member for the Symposium and represented us all at Symposium meetings. Despite being new, *she* should be the big boss in town.

'It should be my job,' she agreed flatly. 'But Willow offered – firmly. The others agreed before I could get a word in edgeways.'

'You may be new to the role, but you tested as the one with the most aptitude out of all of the applicants. And any one of them could have applied – Willow included. You can't let them walk all over you. You have to start as you mean to go on.'

'I know.' She sighed unhappily. 'I didn't want to rock the boat.'

'You need more self-confidence. You have to rock the boat because they need to know it's *your* boat.'

'It doesn't feel like it's my boat.'

Benji scratched his head and joined in the conversation. 'I didn't know anyone was planning on sailing. Is the boat by Portobello beach?'

Bastion snorted quietly. 'It's a metaphorical boat.'

'Ah.'

Kass laughed, too. 'Okay, that helped. I feel better. Oh crap, I'd better go. Willow is coming back in and everyone is glaring at me. I guess no phone calls are allowed when destinies are being made. Talk to you later.' She rang off without a goodbye.

Benji and David stood up. 'We're being summoned.' Benji's eyes flashed white. Without another word, their clothes sank into their skin and they sank into the walls. In moments they were gone.

I frowned. 'Everyone gets to go to the party but us,' I complained to Bastion.

He studied me. 'You want to gatecrash, Bambi?'

'Do you know what? I really do.'

He flashed me a grin. 'Then let's go.'

Chapter 44

I had visions of piling through the door shouting 'I object' at the Council as if I were in some outdated legal drama, but as I approached Benji and David opened it for me. Their bodies were taut with tension and their eyes were glowing white.

'I guess we're expected,' I muttered to Bastion, a frisson of unease shivering down my spine.

'That's a bummer. I really wanted to crash the party.' He sounded disappointed.

'You can smash something later,' I promised.

'Promises, promises,' he teased with a wink. I felt heat rush in his veins and I belatedly realised that my comments could be misconstrued as some crass innuendo. Whoops. I dragged my mind back to the present before it could get too distracted. Now was not the time to be flustered.

I had anticipated having to wheedle my way in front of the Coven Council; friendship or not, I hadn't expected the golems to wave us through. I felt a prickle of unease but I overrode it. I *needed* that list; I needed to know who was a suspect in my Coven. My brain was a feverish whirl of possibilities and it was exhausting. I marched in; I'd deal with any fallout later.

The Coven Council was in session. I was glad to see that nobody was wearing a cowl, though I was surprised to see that only female Council members were there. Where were the men?

When I'd been in this room before, it was poorly lit and ominous; now bright lights were shining almost too brightly. The red carpet had been rolled away to reveal the ancient pentagram. It had been carved painstakingly into the stone flooring. Although its ridges were still clear, it wasn't those that caught my eye but the plethora of runes painted into it. They were dark against the stone but I recognised the tang of blood in the air. Blood runes. They weren't necessarily dark magic, not if the blood had been given willingly, but all the same they were powerful magic.

The room hummed with power rather like the auction house had done, but this power didn't make my teeth hurt. Instead it lifted me up, making me almost giddy and buoyant. I could be swept along by that power so easily if I let it take me. I struggled against it; I needed my wits about me.

Bastion walked next to me, lightly touching my hand, centring me and protecting me because he could feel that I was beguiled by the pull of the room.

The Mother and the Maiden flanked Willow. The three of them started to chant, calling in unison on the Goddess's favour. My scalp prickled.

Swaying, Willow slowly stepped forward. Like Benji and David, her eyes were glowing with a soft white light. I felt another wave of power that wasn't my own and the pull of dizzying magic distracted me again.

Willow turned to me and when she spoke her voice was somehow *more*. 'Come, child. It is your turn to serve.' Her milky-white eyes drilled into me. I had seen eyes like that before when Abigay had communed with the Goddess, and I knew without a doubt that it was not Willow who was speaking to me in that moment. My heart had been galloping like a racehorse, but now it slowed and my breathing took on an unhurried pace. An unnatural calm took a hold of me. The moment hummed.

I took a step towards her but my knees buckled in the face of the overwhelming power that was radiating before me. Bastion was by my side in an instant, catching me before I fell. 'As it should be, Protector,' the Goddess said to Bastion, her tone approving. 'Your life before hers.'

'Yes,' Bastion said simply, as if he wasn't overwhelmed by the presence of a Goddess in our midst. She was the Goddess of the witches, not the griffins, but his tone was deferential; whether she was *his* deity or not, he respected her power.

He helped me forward until I stopped before the Goddess. She smiled; it wasn't Willow's smile, even though it was Willow's lips that curved upwards. The Goddess's smile was like a ray of sunshine beaming on a perfect flower covered in dew.

I frowned. Those florid thoughts couldn't possibly be mine.

A tinkling laugh sounded inside my head. '*Won't you let me have any fun, Amber DeLea?*' the Goddess asked. Her voice in my head was warm, kind and laced with a cheeky humour that made me smile despite myself. I smiled like the moon caressing the dark lands on a winter's night—

Stop it, I thought at her firmly.

Her laughter sounded in my head again. '*As you wish, child of mine.*' She sobered. '*Come then, Amber, and be blessed.*'

Because it seemed right, I curtsied to her. When I rose, she reached out and lifted Abigay's pendant that I'd worn around my neck since her death. The Goddess held it in her elegant fingers. *'Such a beautiful pendant,'* she murmured. 'But it has always been more than a symbol. It is only right that I restore it to its full potential. As it once was, so shall it be.'

Magic pulsed in the room and a bright flash like a solar flare temporarily blinded me. When I opened my eyes, she had laid the pendant against my skin. It was almost unbearably hot. *'Reach up, clasp it with your fingers and know your sisters,'* she murmured.

I had a moment of fear. I'd only had one sister; her name was Becky and she'd tried to kill me. I didn't want sisters *plural* and, if I had to have them, I definitely didn't want to know them.

'Not her,' the Goddess said softly. *'You need not fear her any longer. She faces her own judgement.'*

I jutted my chin. 'I don't fear her,' I stated boldly. I still had nightmares about the bomb that had killed her, though. My bomb.

A smile caressed the Goddess's lips but she didn't call me on the lie. I reached up and touched the amulet gingerly.

'*Hello, Amber,*' murmured a voice in a hundred whispers. My brain struggled to comprehend so many voices speaking at once: it was a roar and it was a whisper, and yet it was silent.

As my fingers grasped the pendant, faces started to flash before my eyes. Woman after woman, some aged, some not, but all with a strength and wisdom that shone in their eyes. Image after image flashed before me and I had the sense of hundreds of women – thousands – through the aeons of time. Each greeted me, '*Hello sister.*'

There were witches from times before there was no date right up to the present day. And finally the last face smiled at me. '*Hello, princess,*' Abigay said gently.

Chapter 45

I fell to my knees and tears flowed freely down my cheeks. I dropped my fingers from the pendant around my neck and turned to Bastion for comfort. He was there instantly, fierce and strong. He partially shifted, losing his T-shirt and used his wings to wrap us in a feathery blanket, offering us precious privacy and blocking us from anyone else's sight.

'I'm okay,' I murmured. 'I'm okay.'

'No, you're not,' he whispered back. 'And that's okay, too.' He clung to me fiercely and I gave a half-laugh and pressed my forehead against his neck. The scent of him was strong there and so reassuring.

When my shocked tears had finally run their course, I pulled back and swiped at my cheeks. I hadn't been prepared to see Abigay, to hear her voice and feel her love, and it had sideswiped me. Joy, disbelief and grief were mingled together inside me.

'*Release her, protector,*' the Goddess ordered gently. '*Our time is not yet done.*'

I nodded and Bastion obeyed, opening his wings and tucking them back into his body where they vanished. He remained shirtless, which distracted me.

'*Focus, Amber.*' The Goddess was amused.

'*Yes, ma'am.*'

'*Welcome to the sisterhood of the Crone, Amber De-Lea.*' The humour was gone from her voice and her tone was ceremonial. '*Your new role is more than a job; it is a new identity, that of a huntress. Fear has no place in your heart. You must be bold. You must stop the rising dark, or the balance will shift forever.*' Her voice was heavy with warning. '*It cannot be borne, Amber. Your sisters will guide you. Heed them. Blessed be.*'

'Blessed be,' I said aloud.

'*You must find Frogmatch. His time grows short,*' she said grimly.

'*Where?*'

'*Seek him in the dead city.*'

'*Where* exactly *in the dead city?*' It was a big place.

I heard her tinkling laugh inside my head. '*If I give you all the answers, your journey will be different. Use your resources and seek him.*' The milky-white light in Willow's eyes faded and she collapsed; the Goddess was gone.

The Mother and the Maiden carefully laid her unconscious body on the floor. The blood on the pentagram had vanished, burned out by the Goddess's presence. The two women turned to me and bowed. 'Blessed be, Crone,' they spoke in unison.

And that was when I realised exactly what had happened. I'd been so wrapped up in the moment, so awed by speaking with the Goddess, that I hadn't fully understood that *I* had been appointed the next Crone.

I was now the unofficial leader of the Coven Council and the guiding voice of the future. If I'd taken time to process it, I'd have freaked out. This was huge, bigger than any of my ambitions. I'd been tasked by the Goddess to stop the rising dark.

The Crone was a position for life. With the gargantuan task of stopping the dark witches, I hoped that mine would last for more than a hot minute.

Chapter 46

The councillors crowded around me, offering congratulations. Seren was decidedly sulky.

'Why aren't the men here?' I asked, genuinely baffled. Why would they willingly miss the Goddess's presence? A ceremony like this happened once in a lifetime; to be on the Council and to choose to miss it was unthinkable.

Seren batted her eyelashes at me. 'It was a moment of *feminine* power.' Her tone said '*duh*'. 'They didn't want to intrude.'

'Who suggested they did not intrude?' I probed.

'Tristan,' Seren pouted. 'Why?'

Because I could only think of only one reason a witch would want to avoid the Goddess and that was because they'd been a very naughty boy.

I didn't answer her question. I was the Crone now, a leader, so I led. We were in the midst of chaos and the witches needed order. I would give them that.

'Take care of Willow – she will need to rest for a number of days. I must leave. The Goddess has laid a task upon me and I must get to it. I will be using the golems. Please let my appointment be known throughout the dead city and Coven-wide. Ready the list of suspects for my perusal and lock down the dead city. No one comes in or out until further notice.' I gave them a brisk nod, turned on my kitten heels and left.

I congratulated myself on my semi-dramatic exit as we went back through the underground passageways. Bastion followed me silently; I sensed no surprise in him at my appointment.

I checked to be sure we had some privacy. Benji and David were a few steps behind us, so I felt able to whisper, 'Why aren't you freaking out?'

Bastion smiled. 'Do you remember Melva's prophecy? *The witch, the Crone, her destiny clear, black witches tremble when she's near. With heart and rune, she'll persevere, a hunt for justice, she'll have no peer. But lurking deep within the night, the Coven's head, her Father's might. A reckoning awaits in close sight, a clash of dark and radiant light.*'

He cleared his throat. 'You're the Crone. You were *always* going to be the Crone. And now you're a huntress.' The pride in his voice made my heart swell. 'We're going to find black witches and kick their asses.'

I was surprised by how much joy and relief his use of 'we' brought me. The task laid on me seemed overwhelming but with Bastion by my side anything seemed possible. I might be the huntress, but he was my weapon.

I turned to Benji and David. 'The Goddess said that Frogmatch doesn't have much time. The black witches have him and we need to locate him – now. I can't run through all of the secret chambers and hidden rooms under the city—'

'—but we can,' Benji interrupted, eyes gleaming at the prospect of helping.

'You can move through the walls and locate Frogmatch without his captor being any the wiser.' I cleared my throat. 'Tristan is my chief suspect. He was the one who excused all of the men from meeting the Goddess, and it was his bodyguard, Mack, who arrested me and threw me in the dungeons. Tristan has been trying to discredit me because for some reason he sees me as a threat, so start your search in his chambers. Check for hidden rooms. Come back here when you locate Frogmatch.'

The two men sank into the walls. The order had slipped out brusquely, which I hadn't intended, but the Goddess's warning had made fear curl in my gut and I never dealt well with fear.

I waited anxiously but Bastion was as calm as ever, an oasis of Zen tranquillity. It was actually quite annoying. At my slightly accusing look, he spoke up. 'Do not underestimate the imp. He'll be fine. Why do you think imps are so often linked to Satan?'

'Because of the red skin and the forked tail?' And the huge claws he'd grown into, and the smell of brimstone?

He shook his head. 'Because, as we saw, they can be dangerous little buggers. The only reason the vampyrs got the imps' tails was because they had enchanted them. Don't write Frogmatch off yet.'

'I haven't, but the Goddess said he doesn't have much time.'

He shrugged. 'She wants us to prioritise him, which we're doing. Worrying solves nothing, Amber.'

I glared. 'Not all of us are stone cold.' As soon as the words left my mouth, I felt his hurt. 'I'm sorry!' I blurted out, stepping closer to him. 'I didn't mean it. You're not cold, not at all. You're caring and kind and wonderful. I'm just worried and I don't handle it well. I'm sorry.'

He studied me and the sting of hurt faded. 'Okay. I didn't mean to demean your worrying, just to alleviate it.'

'I know.' I stepped forward and hugged him, then stood on tiptoe and gave him a soft kiss. 'Hey,' I said brightly. 'Did we just have our first fight? Because that wasn't so bad!'

He smiled and kissed me on the tip of my nose. 'You're so cute.'

'I am not *cute.* Take it back.'

He grinned at me. 'Second fight. We're barrelling through them.'

'Don't be so hasty or we'll miss out on make-up sex,' I quipped.

Bastion smirked. 'We don't want to miss that.' He walked over to Benji's bookcase and pulled a book out. 'This one looks like one of yours,' he commented, passing me the paranormal romance book, *Dry-ad Humping*. I read the blurb with interest, it was a slow-burn romance between a dryad and her loyal gardener.

'It's not an enemies to lovers romance,' I teased Bastion lightly.

'Best put it back then,' he replied with a wink. 'As we know, the best romances are enemies to lovers.'

I put the book down just as Benji burst from the wall. 'We've found him!' he said urgently. 'In a room off Tristan's chambers, just like you thought. I can feel the wards but I couldn't pass through them.'

'Take us there!' I snapped.

David had stepped out, too. He took hold of Bastion whilst Benji took me, and we all sank back into the wall. I fought a shard of fear; Goddess, how I hated travelling like this.

We popped out into a room about twenty seconds later. Twenty long seconds. I shuddered as I sucked in a fresh breath then pulled myself together. We didn't have time for me to be a diva.

I looked around. We were in Tristan's lounge, all polished wooden floors and lush fabrics and pillows. It didn't look like an evil den, but appearances can be deceptive. I touched the walls and used my magic to run through the wards on them. As a reception room, these had wards against vampyrs and a few other helpful ones but nothing sinister.

But I could also see a hidden layer of runes that were not activated – and those were as sinister as hell. Once they lit up, no one would be walking in or out; Tristan could lock this room down like a jail cell. But for now they remained inert. In his arrogance, hiding behind his position as a Council member, he had assumed he was safe.

There was another door, warded to high heaven. I suspected it opened into an office that Tristan used as a dark ritual space.

I touched the wall and the layers of runes lit up as I ran my magic through them. At first glance it looked like they were really heavy-duty but, as I lifted the layers, I spied black runes underneath. Bad things would happen to people who breached those.

I licked my lips. I could start to paint *ezro* but we'd be here forever. I'd have to cancel them, rune by rune, layer by layer. It would take so long and the Goddess's warning had felt urgent.

I didn't know what to do. In desperation, I reached up and clasped my new necklace. *'Sisters, I need help. How do I get through the wards?'*

'Blood,' came the instant answer from a chorus of voices. *'Use the griffin's blood. He can coax down even the black wards with his blood.'*

I turned to Bastion, astonishment on my face. 'You can coax *wards*?'

Chapter 47

My mouth was still open with shock so I clacked it shut. 'How is that possible?' Wards aren't sentient.

No wonder he was the pre-eminent assassin in the world; not even our best wards could hope to keep him out. All those times when I'd strengthened my wards against him, they'd been as ineffectual as a chocolate fireguard.

Bastion cleared his throat. 'A witch uses her magic to draw runes. Each rune could have dozens of uses but it is the witch's intent that dictates how it is used.'

'I know *that,*' I said impatiently. 'I'm a rune master!' He was teaching me to suck eggs.

He gave me a chastening look that I ignored. 'If you'd let me continue...'

I gestured grandly to indicate that the floor was his, then folded my arms and tapped my toes. I managed to restrain the audible huff that wanted to slide out, but only just.

'In giving their intent, the witch gives her magic to the runes and temporarily gives them a purpose. It's not enough to call them sentient but enough that I can disrupt them.'

'Surely the runes don't have the intention to do anything other than what they are wrought to do? You can't coax them to fail.'

'All wards fail – it is a constant cycle. That's why you witches are always having to repaint them. My magic disrupts the link between the rune and their maker, so they fail sooner than they would do otherwise.'

Something connected in my brain. 'Hold on! You once kicked down a door hidden and warded with black runes. You triggered a black-witch's curse and you nearly got *killed*. Why didn't you just coax them down?'

Embarrassment flooded me – Bastion's mortification, not my own. He mumbled something I didn't catch. 'What? Speak up,' I ordered impatiently.

His cheeks were red. 'I was trying to impress you.'

I stared. 'By kicking down a door?'

'Women like that sort of thing,' he muttered.

I struggled not to laugh. 'For future reference, I am far more impressed with your pancake-making skills than your ability to grate cheese with your abs.'

'Good to know.' His face was still red.

'You really pulled a curse down on yourself because you were trying to impress me?'

'Can we leave it now?' he asked plaintively.

I smirked. 'For now, but we're revisiting it later. That really is adorable.'

The deadliest man on seven continents narrowed his eyes. 'I am *not* adorable.'

'You are, but we'll discuss that later. Time is marching on.' I waved my hand impatiently. 'Break the wards, Bastion. Let's rescue our Frogmatch.'

'Yes, ma'am.' He shifted his right hand into talons and raised the pad of his thumb to swipe across the claw. When blood welled and he touched it to the door, the wards lit up so brightly I had to look away. Layer upon layer of them blazed across my retina then, just as suddenly, they melted away and almost dribbled down the walls.

'I didn't do it with finesse,' Bastion apologised. 'I've just ripped away the ones from the entrance, so we still need to be careful. Tristan may be alerted to some of his wards being destroyed.'

'Let him come,' I said grimly. 'We'll be waiting.'

Chapter 48

I painted *perthro*, the revelation rune, on the door just to be sure all the wards at the entrance had been broken. Not that I didn't trust Bastion, but he *had* blundered into black wards before and I wasn't leaving anything to chance. I couldn't bear the thought of seeing him broken and exhausted like that again. Of course this time I'd be a damned sight quicker about lifting any curses, but getting the blood of the witch that had painted black runes always made things tricky.

We couldn't be sure that it was Tristan who had painted them – it could have been his acolyte or another lackey. It was important never to assume anything about runes and I hadn't checked the magical signature before Bastion had ripped them down, an oversight I was annoyed about.

When nothing lit up on the *perthro*, I nodded. 'All clear,' I said to Bastion. I tried to turn the door handle but the office door was locked, albeit with a good old-fashioned key this time. 'Locked.' I frowned. 'Can you open it?'

Jinx had a set of lockpicks and the skills to use it, but I had no such skill. Doubtless Bastion did. 'I've got a key,' he said calmly. Without changing expression, he reared back and kicked a heavy foot against the lock. The door flung open.

I felt a small surge of desire. Okay, kicking down doors was a *little* impressive. Stupid cavewoman hormones. I battened down the flare of desire; now was definitely not the time to get distracted. Bastion sent me a smirk and a wink. He'd felt it. Dammit.

As I swept past him into the room, horror slammed into me. The room was lined with cages and rank with the stench of faeces, blood and death.

'Ellie!' Frogmatch coughed, doubled over in his small prison. 'Tristan is a black witch!' He was coughing and his red skin was already turning pink, a sure sign that he was ill.

I smiled at my little imp. 'We figured. Let's get you out of here,' I glanced around the room. 'All of you.'

I opened my tote and grabbed a jar of revelation potion and a paintbrush. I painted *perthro* but no runes showed up; the imp was locked away with nothing but the metal bars on his prison. Iron, no doubt.

'I have something to tell you, Ellie,' Frogmatch said. 'I should have told you earlier. When I was snooping in your Coven, I heard a man talking about controlling vampyrs.'

I froze. 'A necromancer?' Was it the one that had killed Melva?

'That's what I'm figuring.' He gave a little cough. 'I couldn't hear the other side of the conversation. He must have been on the phone.'

'It was definitely a man?' I yanked on the cage door with all my might. It shuddered but didn't give way; another pull should do it.

'Yes, definitely a man.'

'Did you see him? Can you identify him?' I braced one hand against the cage and pulled the door again. This time it gave way and I reached in and gently lifted Frogmatch out of confinement. His body was terrifyingly cool to the touch. I cradled him close.

He coughed again. 'No, but if I heard his voice again, I'm sure I could.'

'Okay, this is good. Thank you, Frogmatch.'

'I should have told you earlier but we were flying to Edinburgh against the clock.' He took a shuddering breath.

'If I'd died, you wouldn't have known you had a necromancer in your midst.'

'I've had a pretty good idea for a while,' I admitted. 'But I didn't know that they were male. Thank you, that narrows the suspect pool a lot.' And in my head it confirmed who the necromancer was. 'Let's get you healed up,' I said firmly.

'Help the others,' he argued faintly. I grimaced but, looking around, I could see he wasn't the worst off, not by a long shot. I set Frogmatch down carefully and turned to the rest of the cages. There were all sorts of small creatures in them: imps, cats, fairies, mice, all of them missing parts of their bodies.

I felt sick. I didn't know whether their limbs had been cut off to be used in potions or if they'd been hurt for their pain to power black runework, but either way it was horrific.

'Benji, David,' I called desperately. 'A little help.'

When the golems walked in and saw the imprisoned creatures, they let out a roar of outrage. 'This is not right,' David snarled.

'It is not,' Benji agreed. 'We will help them.'

We searched the room for keys but found none. I patiently painted a *perthro* on each of the other cages but found no runes on them – utter laziness on Tristan's part. Bastion, Benji and David started ripping them open with brute force.

A lot of the creatures were malnourished and could barely lift their heads even when they were gently cradled out of their confinement. The cats and mice appeared to be ordinary creatures; there was no familiar magic that I could sense.

The imps and fairies were as ashen as Frogmatch, and many of them weren't moving. I had no idea how long they had been caged for but I was betting it was a long while. Too long. I felt a wave of fury. Most of them were too far gone to help but we had to try – we might save one or two, but not many more. The imps' tails had been removed, their red skin was washed out, barely a faint pink. Next to them, Frogmatch looked the picture of health.

The fairies stared at us, unmoving; their wings had been torn off. They had retreated into the safety of their own minds. I had no idea if I could regrow the wings until I examined them properly; for now, we had to get the fairies to safety and give them food and water. Sometimes potions are no replacement for the basics like food and rest.

Benji had the cats and mice cradled in his arms. Even though they were half-starved, none of the cats twitched so much as a hair at being so close to the mice, their natural prey. They were lethargic and unmoving. So many living beings harmed – and for what?

David gently got the fairies out, carrying their tiny bodies effortlessly in his huge hands. Bastion did the same to the imps. 'Take them to the awakening room,' I suggested. 'It's closer and there will be plenty of healing potions there.'

Bastion hesitated at the threshold. 'Go!' I barked. 'They need healing! Hurry! I'll be just behind you.'

He felt the truth of the words and left. I painted the revelation rune *perthro* again and lit up the remaining runes in the office. This time, I studied the magical signature; it was probably Tristan's, but I wanted to know if it wasn't.

Bastion had melted away most of the runes but some still remained, and those were far too dangerous to leave unattended. The runes in the lounge had been hidden but the dark runes in the office were there to be seen – and activated. If someone stumbled in here and activated them by accident, I'd have never forgiven myself. Tristan wanted there to be dire consequences to interlopers. Bastion had ripped open a path for us but several live bombs remained. It would take a few minutes to cancel them all but it was worth the effort.

When I had subdued the worst of the black runes, I looked around. The office was filled with cages, knives and other implements of torture and the carpet was covered in suspiciously dark stains.

Horrified, I shook my head. I would stop practices like this; I had given the Goddess my word but now I swore it again to myself. I would stop at nothing to end this. Nothing.

Chapter 49

I headed out of the office and into the lounge but stopped abruptly as I crossed the threshold. Three things immediately alarmed me: firstly, Tristan was sprawled arrogantly on his sofa, his gaze pinned to me; secondly, his living-room door was shut and the layer of sleeping wards had been awakened and activated, and thirdly, there was a new rug on his floor. I doubted it was there because he'd felt the sudden urge to decorate. Goddess knew what active runes were hidden under it. He must have gone into the room seconds after Bastion had left it.

The runes shone on his walls; he must have just reactivated them. Dammit, why had I spent so long deactivating the office ones? I should have dealt with these runes too. I felt a frisson of fear as I examined them. That would teach me to lollygag behind.

I had walked straight into Tristan's trap. I was imprisoned here unless he kindly stood still whilst I painted *ezro* on all his runes, which somehow I doubted he would. Being confined was reviving all sorts of prison memories for me but, unluckily for Tristan, those memories were kicking in my flight-or-fight reflex. With flight impossible, that only left one thing to do.

'Amber,' he greeted me.

'You're a bastard,' I spat back. 'A monster. How could you do that to all those poor creatures?'

He laughed. 'I've done far worse. Don't be so naïve.' His voice was condescending. 'Where's your pet griffin now, hmm?' He looked at me with undisguised glee.

But there were things he didn't know. Bastion was my familiar and we were bonded; even now my griffin was feeling my fear and panic and was no doubt heading straight back to me. And Bastion could rip through wards like anyone else could rip through paper. And I still had my athame in my ankle holster hidden under my swishy skirt.

I gave a hard tug on my bond and let Bastion feel the edge of panic that I was feeling from being trapped. I felt a rush of emotion roll back – anger mostly – and I knew that he was already on his way to me. He'd only been a minute, maybe two, ahead of me. I just needed to keep

Tristan busy, and I didn't think that would be difficult. He had a huge ego and, much as I didn't want to stroke anything of Tristan's, I'd do it if it kept me alive.

'Your father protects you, you know? Pathetic really,' he taunted, 'You're not one of us and you never will be. Honestly, Amber, healing creatures for *free*? How pathetic can you get! You're the laughing stock of *all* witches, not just the black ones.'

I smiled tightly. 'And yet I bet none of you have the balls to mock me to my father's face.'

That wiped the smile right off *his* face. 'I've wanted to put you in your place for *years*,' he snarled. 'What a fucking delight it was shoving you in that cell. And Mack wasn't too gentle, was he? I told him my suspicions about you. He'll definitely alibi me when I claim we walked in and found you already dead.'

He pushed up from the sofa and drew a wicked-looking blade from its scabbard. He was trying to get me to back onto the pentagram that was under the rug. But I'd seen the room before the rug had appeared and I wasn't an idiot. Besides, stepping back from him wasn't the answer here.

'I'm going to slice you into little pieces, Amber DeLea.' His smile had an edge of madness.

I reached up and grasped my amulet. *Anyone know any-thing about knife fighting?'* I asked, a shade desperately.

'I've got you,' one of the voices murmured. *'Relinquish hold.'*

'Relinquish hold of what?'

'Yourself.' She shoved me aside forcefully. Suddenly my hands were moving but I was no longer driving my own body.

I didn't fight the sensation. The Goddess had gifted me the amulet and the spirits that resided in it; besides, Tristan's knife was really big and if I wasn't careful, I'd get really dead.

She – her name was Edith, though I didn't know how I knew that – drew my athame from my ankle holster. Tristan laughed aloud. 'Amber, Amber, Amber. We both know you don't know how to wield that, honey.' His voice dripped with condescension.

He was right, I didn't – but Edith sure did. She moved my body with a precision I had never felt before, tipping me onto the balls of my feet, spreading my legs in a stance that I recognised as a fighting one.

Tristan snickered again then stepped forward, knife slashing towards me. Edith spun me effortlessly out of the way. Then, with a leap and a swirl of my skirts, I was *behind*

Tristan. He whirled around, startled and off balance, and Edith made me kick him solidly in the balls.

He let out an agonised yowl and staggered back into his own pentagram trap. He didn't realise at first what had happened and lunged towards me again, blade high, before he bounced off his own containment wards. He hadn't wanted me to wriggle out of them so he'd done a solid job of drawing them up. He wasn't incompetent, just evil, and now he was trapped in a prison of his own making. He could undo the runes, of course, but it would take time.

I nudged Edith and she willingly relinquished hold of me and sank back into the amulet. I glared at Tristan. 'Don't call me honey.'

'What the fuck?' He gaped at me.

The door exploded with such force that chunks of wood flew off its frame. Bastion stormed in, rage roaring through him with such strength that I felt my own anger rise. The closer we were, the more I felt his emotions; if I'd thought he was angry before, now I knew that anger was a mere trickle compared to this torrent.

He gave a screech that shouldn't have come out of a human mouth. The pentagram that held Tristan had been designed to hold an enemy in place, not to stop a new threat from coming in, so he had no defence against Bastion except his knife – which was suddenly looking far smaller than it had a moment ago.

Bastion shifted into griffin form, closed the distance to Tristan and promptly ripped his throat out. Blood sprayed across the walls.

I sighed. 'I had him contained,' I grumped. 'I was going to *question* him.'

Bastion shifted into human form, pushed me against the nearest wall and kissed me furiously. 'He had you *trapped.* I felt your fear. I let you down.' His anger was unabated but this time it was directed inwards.

'Hey, none of that! I sent you ahead of me to help the imps. If I hadn't dawdled to remove the wards none of this would have happened. I won't let you blame yourself.'

'You won't *let* me?' His voice was incredulous.

I raised my chin and looked into his golden eyes. 'You heard me, griffin. I won't *let* you. I do not accept your anger.' I slid a hand around the back of his neck, 'I will, however, accept your ardour.'

I pulled his head down and kissed him until his blood sang with something other than rage. Something much more fun.

Chapter 50

'We're making progress,' I said confidently to the assembled Council. 'I have rooted out yet another black witch among us – on the Council itself.'

I looked each of the members in the eye. 'I have been appointed by the Goddess to root out this infestation and I take my duties seriously. If you are a black witch, know that I *will* find you.'

I let the threat hang in the air for a long minute. I didn't know for certain whether there were more black witches on the Council. With Hilary and Tristan dead and whoever had been impersonating Felix removed, the Council was in a better – and worse – shape than it had been for some time.

'Your days are numbered,' I continued. 'Hilary and Tristan are dead. You will be next.' I noted with interest that all the councillors held my gaze except for Seren, but that could simply be because of our personal history.

I cleared my throat. 'It's time for a re-brand. Too often we shy away from calling people or their actions evil but they are. To gain power from torture and death – that *is* evil.'

I thought of Abigay and her dark skin. I didn't want ever to describe her with the same descriptor as *them*. 'We're not calling them "black witches" any more. We're calling them what they really are: "evil witches". That is what they are because that is what they are doing. If you are evil I will find you and I will see you culled from the Coven.'

The Other is a dog-eat-dog world and too often the witches are seen as the Chihuahua of the realm: yappy, but with no bite. Well, I was bringing the bite back.

'I want all witches to carry an athame and a potion bomb at all times. If you are on the streets, you are armed. Whether we have accepted it or not, we're at war. Let it be known that there will be no mercy. There will be no Connection trial.' I had expected applause but instead the Council members stared at me, shellshocked.

'No waiting for six months to fill the Council vacancies.' I said after a beat when it became obvious no acknowledgment would be forthcoming. 'This week you do a UK

Coven-wide email notifying anyone who is interested in becoming part of the Council that they must come to Edinburgh to undergo testing. We are going to get stronger – and we are going to do it *now*.'

Well, that was it: I guessed rousing speeches weren't in my wheelhouse. I thought I'd done a good job but there was no standing ovation. I gave them a sharp nod and started to move off the podium.

Kass started to clap and slowly the others joined in. It wasn't quite the thunderous applause I'd hoped for, but it was a start. I left them to it: the Crone was supposed to guide, not micromanage. Who was going to organise the email and how they were going to co-ordinate the testing was for them to arrange.

Look at me! I was delegating! I felt a tiny bit proud of myself. Then I felt a warm tingle, like a burst of sun on my skin, and I knew that the Goddess approved wholeheartedly of what I'd started.

Bastion followed me out of the Council chamber. I closed the door behind us and paused. Benji and David were both standing to attention, guarding the entrance. I studied them. 'I could use a hand,' I said finally. 'But I don't want to separate you or take you away from your post if you'd rather stay. I need people I can trust around me, people I *know* aren't evil. I know you two aren't.'

The golems exchanged glances then David bowed. 'I thank you for your words and consideration. If it pleases you, Crone, I will serve the Council as that was my awakened purpose.'

I nodded. 'It is right,' I agreed.

Benji stepped up to me. 'I would love to serve you, Crone.' He gave a low bow.

The title made my heart clench. 'Not from you,' I whispered as I pulled him upright. 'It is Am Bam to you, always.' According to the rules, the Crone's family could retain and use her given name.

His smile was like the rising of the sun; his joy lit up the room as he pulled me into his arms. 'Am Bam,' he murmured, kissing my forehead. His cold hard arms encircled me. Cold or not, he truly gave the best hugs. He released me. 'Where are we going?'

I sighed. 'To clean out another black witch.' He looked at me expectantly. 'We're going home,' I explained grimly.

Chapter 51

'You're not leaving without me!' a small voice piped up. Frogmatch.

I turned to the little imp, noting with relief that his skin had darkened back to his signature red. Food, rest and potions had done him the world of good. He shot up from the floor, moved past Benji's intricately tied shoelaces, scrambled up his legs and swung onto the golem's shoulder.

With Benji's height, I only had to crane my head a little to make eye contact with the impertinent imp. I told him he was looking much better. 'Thanks to you, Ellie,' he said solemnly. His jaw worked. 'Not all the others were so lucky. Thank you, though, for forcing the Council to heal as many of us as possible without charging anyone.'

'It's only right,' I said firmly. 'It was our mess to clean up.' I realised as soon as I said it that calling the abduction, torture, maiming and death of dozens of creatures a 'mess' was inaccurate and highly insensitive. I winced internally. 'I just meant—' I started.

'I know what you meant,' Frogmatch interrupted with a wan smile. 'It's okay. But if you're off to confront another black witch, I'm coming with you.'

'Evil witch,' I corrected him absentmindedly.

'What?'

'We're not using the term "black witch" any more. It makes them less evil, less offensive, and it's too easy to start on the slippery slope of grey witchdom. Saying "white witches" and "black witches" just makes it seem like they are on opposing sides, but it is more than that. So we're calling them what they are.'

Frogmatch conjured up a smile which had none of its usual joviality. 'You're re-branding evil, huh?'

'Just calling them what they are,' I repeated firmly. 'No more of this fifty shades of grey.'

'From the contents of your bookcase,' Frogmatch muttered. 'I thought you were a fan of *Fifty Shades*.' I felt myself flush. Great: even my imp knew about my romance-book addiction. I levelled him with a glare. I wasn't ashamed of my book choices.

'Whether I like it or not, you shouldn't yuck someone else's yum,' I said firmly. 'Your kink may not be my kink, and that's okay.'

He blinked and tried to find his footing again. 'I'm just saying, I'm totally okay if you want to spank me.'

Bastion let out a low threatening growl. I'd never heard that sound from him before – an eagle screech, yes, but not his lion's growl.

Frogmatch blanched. 'Sorry, your growliness,' he blathered. 'Of course she is your witch to spank or not spank. You know, whatever floats your boat.'

'Frogmatch,' I sighed. 'Stop talking.'

'You know, I sense that maybe I should.'

I grinned. 'So you're coming with us to confront evil?'

'Yes, ma'am, I am. And I want to spit in its eye.'

I met his gaze and found that I wasn't inclined to deny him. He'd been through hell and back; if he wanted to spread around some bodily fluids, who was I to say no?

'Can we address the you-growing-huge thing?' I asked. He started to quirk an eyebrow and I knew that an innuendo was coming. I held up my hand. 'No. I did leave that open, but *no*. We're talking seriously, as adults.'

'My response was going to be very adult,' he huffed.

'No.'

He sighed. 'Imps can grow in size in emergencies. It's a secret. It's not done often or lightly.'

'Because?'

'Because it can kill us. You felt how cold I was.'

'I did. I assumed it was because of the imprisonment.'

'No, it was because of the engorgement.'

'*Engorgement*. Seriously?'

He flashed me a toothy grin. 'That's what we call it.'

'Of course you do,' I muttered. 'Fine. You can come, but absolutely no ... engorging.'

Looking a little more like his old self, Frogmatch smirked triumphantly. 'I'll just stay here on this piece of rock,' he patted Benji on the shoulder.

Benji looked rather pleased to have his own personal devil on his shoulder. Bastion sent Frogmatch a glower; I don't think he'd enjoyed the imp's spanking quips all that much.

I stood. 'Fine. Let's go – all of us.' What a motley crew we made but, motley or not, we were deadly. The evil witch in my Coven wouldn't know what had hit them.

Chapter 52

When I'd been at the evil Coven's soul auction, they had talked about their familiars and about their sickness. That had sent up a red flag straight away, one I'd been trying to pull back down ever since.

I hadn't seen Jeb's familiar, Jessica, around the Coven tower in weeks. Sure, it could be a coincidence, but... Frogmatch had said the necromancer was a male and Jeb had been on the scene incredibly fast after our first ogre attack. And he was the only other person who had known that we were going to meet the Seer High Priestess, Melva, the day that she'd been murdered. Plus, we'd been attacked soon after leaving the venue.

I had tried to deny it because the whole idea made my stomach turn. Not Jeb; surely not Jeb. But the more I thought about it, the more the idea had taken root. Jeb was a mid-level witch, yet he hadn't looked slightly tired after breaking the ancient clearing on me. And that look on his face when he realised Bastion and I were together? I'd written it off as jealousy in the heat of the moment, but the truth was it had been *malevolent.*

All I had were my suspicions and my gut instinct. Bastion didn't ask who my suspect was, but maybe he didn't need to.

As much as it stuck in my craw, I used Tristan's trick. I prepared the pentagram in my living room with truth runes, covered them with the rug then I called Jeb to my room to 'do a handover' now that I was back from Edinburgh.

I had used truth runes as well as containment runes judiciously in the hidden pentagram. I planned to offer Jeb some refreshments and hold out a mug so he'd have to step across the rug to take it. It wasn't the most elaborate sting operation, but there's a reason the adage 'Keep It Simple Stupid' exists.

Realising it probably wasn't wise to keep my suspicions to myself, I blurted abruptly, 'I think Jeb is evil.' It sounded strange to say it aloud.

Oscar blanched. 'Jeb? What makes you think that?'

'A few things. His familiar has been absent from the tower for weeks. He was too quick to come to the scene after the ogre attack. He was one of the few who knew we were visiting Melva. If I'm wrong, I'll apologise to him.' But I was sure that I wasn't wrong. That flash of fury I'd seen in him had been dark, more than that of a man scorned.

There was a knock at the door: Jeb had arrived. I struggled to keep my face impassive and touched my necklace, not for a solution to a problem but for support. I wanted to be wrong with all my heart. I had trusted Jeb for years; he'd been my right-hand man, my confidant. If he was evil, my judgement had been way off – and I loathe being wrong.

Oscar opened the door as I busied myself making tea for us all. 'Hi Jeb,' I called as casually as I could. 'Come on in.'

'Is Ethan coming, too?' he asked as he strolled in.

'We're doing a separate handover for him,' I lied smoothly.

'Making sure the notes tally?' he joked.

'Just to ensure we get your individual impressions about how things are going. Milk no sugar, right?'

'Yes, please.'

I held out the mug to him and he stepped forward, carefully skirting the rug. I might not have noticed that in a normal meeting, but I noticed it now. Jeb knew I had a permanent pentagram there – heck, he'd helped paint it.

My stomach lurched with dread. If Jeb was innocent, there was no reason to skirt a pentagram, even a hidden one. My face fell, even as he took the mug from me. The mug read: *Careful, I'm an evil genius*, but he wasn't looking at the words. Instead he was studying my oh-so-expressive face.

I saw knowledge dawn on his face. 'Ah,' he said calmly. 'The cat is out of the bag, then.'

It turned out that I didn't need the truth runes after all. 'Why Jeb? Why?' I asked, needing desperately to understand. 'You killed Cindy and took her tail? Arranged Melva's death? Why? Why turn to necromancy? Help me understand.'

As he set down the mug, his eyes flicked to Bastion, Benji and Oscar. The latter had a lighter in his hands, flame exposed, ready to flambé him. I saw the moment that Jeb accepted that he wasn't escaping. And that made him even more dangerous.

'Help you understand? Why? So you can pity me and my choices? I pity *you*, Amber,' he said forcefully. 'Your mind is so closed. If you would open yourself up to the possibility of darker power, you could be great.'

'No,' I said firmly. 'Never.' Never again.

'Pain is a great resource, Amber,' he tried again. 'When I broke that clearing on your mind, the magic didn't take it's toll on me, instead, it gifted me with strength from your pain. I was buzzing with power afterwards.'

The thought that he'd used my pain for his own gain made me feel faintly sick. And I wasn't the only one whose pain he'd used. He'd removed Cindy's tail and killed her. A familiar! 'Goddess, Jeb, it's so wrong. How could you do that to Cindy?'

He shrugged. 'Something in black-magic use is making our familiars sick. No matter what you think of us, we love our familiars. Madame X is making potions to keep them going. She needs tails and the pain of their removal whilst the familiars are still alive. I was instructed to harvest a tail. Ria had made her about-turn known but there's no leaving the black Coven, not ever. Ria had to be told that. If a picture is worth a thousand words, then a mutilation is worth a million. So ... Cindy.'

'Why not harm Ria's familiar, Fido?' Fido was a small brown mouse that often lived in Ria's pocket.

'The death of her mother's familiar was sufficient punishment. The black Coven demands strength – we wouldn't willingly make one of our own weak by removing their familiar, even to give them a lesson. Better to kill a family member's.' His tone was matter of fact. No doubt it would also have been tricky to separate Ria from Fido.

'That's insane,' I muttered, horrified that anyone could even contemplate harming or killing a familiar as punishment. It was wrong on every level.

'Letting insubordination go unpunished is insane,' he countered. 'I even got to clean up the scene.' He smirked. 'I took the blood-soaked carpet from the scene of her death because that held pain that could be used.' His smirk turned vicious. 'And it wasn't even Cindy's body that we cremated because I'd given it to Madame X for parts. Your oh-so-touching eulogy was for a stuffed toy cat.'

Horror clawed at me; depriving Cindy of her final rites was monstrous. 'You're evil,' I whispered. 'What other horrors have you committed?'

'Too many to name,' he said honestly.

'Killing Melva – that was you?'

He nodded. 'Yes, but that was because I was ordered to. Nothing personal.'

Rage flared in me. 'Why?'

'To keep you from learning about the prophecy, of course.'

'And how do you know about that?'

'Your father knew about its existence but he also knew you mustn't hear it. Steps had to be taken.'

Unfortunately for them, I *had* heard it. They'd killed Melva too late, but they didn't need to know that. 'And the attacks on my mother, on me? Were those "nothing personal", too?'

He waved away my words. 'The attacks on your mum were never serious. They were a distraction for you. She was safe, she had griffin protectors.' His expression turned a tad wistful. 'I had a plan, Amber. I was going to woo you, make you fall in love with me. Your father would have seen me as his son-in-law and I could have inherited his whole empire. You don't know what it's like Amber, being a male in a matriarchal society. There are no coven fathers, Amber.'

'Oh boo hoo,' I snapped. 'The UK is still a patriarchal society. Men are still paid more than women. There are only 34% of women as directors of top FTSE 100 companies. The glass ceiling is alive and well. Witches may be matriarchal, but our society isn't. Don't expect me to cry a river. And besides, there may not be coven fathers, but we have men on the coven council too, just as many as we have women.'

He looked at me with exasperation. 'But there's no male Crone, no male equivalent of the Triune. The Leader is going to change all of that. You'll see.' He sighed and ran a hand through his hair. 'You never saw me as anything other than dear, harmless Jeb, did you? I didn't stand a chance. I waited too long, overdid the kindness routine. I thought I had time, but you had me friend-zoned. If you didn't come round in a year or two, there are plenty of enchanted artefacts that would have made you fall in love with me, but the Leader was against that. I couldn't risk his disapproval. If I could just have won you over, he would have been so pleased.'

Jeb huffed out a breath. '

You made me fail him.' He glared at me and gestured towards Bastion. 'If I'd known you were into bestiality I would have moved faster. Fucking a creature Amber? Really?'

Bastion's growl was low and threatening and I felt his anger rising. Jeb's answering smirk was triumphant. Bastion took a step toward him. 'Stop!' I ordered. 'He's goading you. He *wants* you to kill him. We saw how the evil Coven deals with those that fail.'

Jeb ignored my jab and smiled as he taunted Bastion. 'Yes, stop. Like a good little guard dog. Woof-woof.'

'You attacked my mum,' I interjected, trying to bring the focus back to the interrogation.

He shrugged. 'Not seriously, only enough to divert attention. She wasn't harmed – we just needed her to be moved from the home she was in. The griffins guarding her were more than a match for the vampyrs I sent.'

'Why did you need her to be moved?'

'Why? So that we could recover the harkan crystal from her room, of course.'

I felt the room closing in on me. 'What? Why would Mum have the harkan crystal?'

His smirk was dark, twisted and full of schadenfreude. 'Because she was its latest creator.'

'You're lying,' I spat.

'Am I? Your mum isn't roses and kittens, Amber. Why do you think she went to the Third realm so much?'

'To be there for me, to raise me.'

He laughed. 'Poor Amber, so delusional. Do you think your mother is stupid? Why would she risk her sanity for something so inane? No. She was trying to undo her so-called crimes. But some things can't be undone, no matter how hard you try.'

I looked at Oscar. He was glaring at Jeb but his eyes were resigned. 'It can't be true,' I breathed. 'Oscar, tell me it isn't true.' He said nothing and my heart broke.

While we were distracted, Jeb pulled a knife from his ankle holster. He threw himself at me, the blade raised. But Bastion wasn't distracted; Bastion is never distracted. Jeb was only two steps from me when Bastion's talons tore through his throat. Crimson blood sprayed over me as he collapsed inches from me, staining my rug.

So Jeb had got his death by griffin after all, I thought dully. At least this time Bastion had let me question my erstwhile assistant before he'd meted out his own permanent brand of justice.

Chapter 53

I showered off Jeb's blood whilst Bastion and Benji disposed of his body via a quick trip to the Coven incinerator. As I stepped out of the shower, I felt clean but utterly lost.

Oscar had made me an orange juice and he held it out to me, looking uncertain. I stared at it but didn't take it. 'You knew? You knew she'd used black magic?'

Frustration was visible in every line of his body. 'It's not like you think. What she did was for the greater good, Amber. She's a good woman.'

'She used evil magic. Yes or no?'

He grimaced then nodded. 'Yes. As did you, once,' he pointed out softly.

The wind went out of my sails. 'Yes,' I sighed. 'I did – when I was young and stupid.' I had saved Jake's life using black runes, brought him back from the brink of death, but he had never been the same. I had often blamed the black magic, the runes, but I should never have painted them on him. I should have let him die, but at the time I couldn't.

'Your mother was young once, too,' he murmured. 'She was trying to do what was right.'

'The end doesn't justify the means.'

'Doesn't it? That's a question for each of us and our own measure of what is right and wrong.'

'Can you tell me what she did?'

He shook his head, 'She made me swear—'

'—an oath.' I sighed. Mum sure did love her oaths.

I had seen first-hand with Abigay what the cost of breaking one of Mum's oaths was: death. So, although it half-killed me, I didn't press Oscar.

The silence that stretched between us was tense and heavy, its weight like an anvil on my chest. My heart hurt and I suspected Oscar's did too. I didn't want that for him; it wasn't his fault.

I'd been meaning to raise something and now seemed like the perfect time so I broke the silence. 'I saw you.'

'What?' he asked, confused. 'When?'

'When Jeb broke the clearing on my mind. I was focusing on recovering forgotten memories from my father. Some of the memories given back to me were the ones that had been cleared from me, but others were forgotten ones. Forgotten memories of my *other* father – forgotten memories of you. I remembered you brushing my hair for school and putting it in a plait. I remembered you doing maths homework with me at the dining room table. I remembered you sitting with me while I practised my runes.'

I cleared my throat. 'From the moment you entered my life, blood relative or not, you were always there for me. I want you to know how much I appreciate that, Oscar. How much I appreciate *you*.'

His eyes filled with tears and he looked away so I couldn't see them. 'Hey,' I said firmly, 'don't be ashamed of your tears. You're allowed to have big emotions too.' I was channelling Bastion.

He swallowed hard and looked at me nervously. 'For the longest time I've wanted to ask you something.'

'Anything,' I said simply. Oscar had killed ogres by char-grilling them, flung flames around like a pyrotechnician, defended me against all and sundry – yet now he looked uneasy. 'Anything,' I reiterated firmly, touching his hand.

'If you'd like to – and you don't have to – but if you'd like to it would be okay with me if you wanted to call me Dad. Sometimes. Not all the time, of course – you're older now. And only if you want to. I wish I'd said something when you were younger, but I didn't want you to think I was trying to replace your father.' He was rambling, anxious about my reaction.

My vision swam with tears and a rock took up residence in my throat. I gripped his hand more firmly and nodded. 'I'd love to … Dad.'

He nodded back and suddenly both of us were fighting tears. The absurdity of it made me choke out a half-laugh. We were ridiculous; this wasn't a hand-holding situation. I stepped closer for a hug. He took me in his arms and kissed me lightly on the forehead.

After several long minutes of silence he said, 'Should we visit your mum?'

'What's the point?' I asked, my voice hitching with despair. 'She hasn't known either of us in days. Her condition is worsening suddenly and I don't know why.'

Oscar's face tightened as he sighed and stepped back. He knew why. If I wanted the truth out of Mum, I needed to speak to her and the only way I could do that was to heal her fractured mind. I had tried so many potions but I'd been trying to achieve the wrong thing. I had focused on curing mental illnesses when what I needed was to heal the temporal rift in her mind. Nothing like a tall order.

Luckily, I had some ideas.

Oscar brushed some stray hairs out of my eyes. 'The point is to go there and love her. Even if she doesn't know you, she'll know that she's not alone and that's worth a little heartache for us.'

He was absolutely right. 'Thank you,' I said. 'For everything. But now I need some time alone. You visit Mum, if you want to. I'll visit her soon, I promise. I want to – I *need* to. I know you're right.' He *was* right. It was always worth the heartache to see her; even if she didn't know me, I knew *her*, and being with her buoyed me up even on the hard days.

Oscar kissed my cheek and went to the door. 'I'll stay outside until Bastion is back.' I didn't bother to argue.

Alone, I went into my bedroom and opened the cupboard to my safe. 'What are you doing, Ellie?' Frogmatch's voice piped up, making me jump.

'The impossible,' I answered grimly.

Chapter 54

'Stay quiet,' I instructed Frogmatch. 'Grimmy is a bit–'
bigoted? '–dated in his views.'

'Not a fan of imps, huh?'

'Nor any sort of creature,' I admitted. 'As I said … dated.'

I stroked a finger down Grimmy's spine but nothing happened. With a reluctant grimace, I pricked my forefinger using the point of my athame until blood welled. When I stroked the spine with the fresh blood, the book came to life.

Grimmy floated upwards and glowed lightly. His pages fluttered, like he was stretching. 'Why, Miss Amber! To what do I owe this pleasure?'

'I need a potion to heal a temporal rift in someone's mind. Do you know of such a thing?'

He fluttered, flustered. 'Miss Amber, no such potion exists!'

'As far as you know,' I countered.

'If it existed, I'd know,' he said firmly. 'If you want that potion, you need to make it for yourself.'

I didn't have time for that. The irony wasn't lost on me. 'A healing base, a pewter cauldron. Milk of thistle, fennel, damson leaf. What else?'

Grimmy was still agitated. 'There is nothing to be done,' he said reluctantly. 'There is no ingredient for time, Miss Amber.' And that was where he was wrong.

I called Tom Smith, Emory's right-hand man. 'Crone,' he answered, his tone respectful. As usual, there was nothing wrong with the dragons' information network. My new position had barely been announced in Edinburgh yet Tom was already in the know.

'Tom, Jinx took Gato with her on honeymoon. Did she take Indy?' It was a long shot and I held my breath as I waited for his answer. Indy and Gato are hellhounds and they can manipulate the realms – including the Third realm that controls time. If there was any ingredient to represent time, it would come from a hellhound.

'No.' I could hear the grimace in Tom's voice. 'Jinx felt like she was a little untrained to take on honeymoon. She was worried Indy would destroy the hotel rooms.' From what I'd seen of the pup, that was a valid concern.

'Can I speak to her?'

'Jinx?'

'Indy.'

There was a beat of silence. 'Sure,' he said finally. 'Why not? Though I don't guarantee you'll get much sense out of her.'

I didn't need to understand the hellhound, I just needed her to understand me. I contemplated calling Lucy for help. As a piper she can talk to animals, which would come in handy, but I hesitated. She would do anything for a friend, even if it was to her detriment, but she had visiting werewolves to deal with. No, I couldn't distract her now when she needed her wits about her. I cared about her too much to derail her career.

Indy would understand me just fine; hellhounds are very smart. 'Where is Indy?' I asked Tom.

'At the castle.' Caernarfon Castle is the dragons' stronghold; there is a reason why the dragon appears on the Welsh flag.

'I'm on my way.' I hung up and stowed Grimmy back in the safe. When I left the bedroom, Bastion was pacing outside the bedroom door.

'Hey,' I greeted him, stepping into his arms. He smelled like sandalwood and something uniquely him. He'd just showered – he'd probably been splattered with Jeb's blood, too. It wasn't a pleasant thought.

'Hey, Bambi,' he murmured. 'I'm sorry I killed him. I know you wanted to question him, but I couldn't risk you.' He was braced for a fight.

I sighed and rested my head against his chest. 'I know. Jeb did it on purpose – he didn't want to be captured, to be a liability to his foul Coven. I don't think it was fanatical loyalty that made him do it but fear of the evil witches and what they'd do to him.'

'Maybe. All the same, I'm sorry. I know you liked him.'

'It looks like I didn't even know him. The Jeb I *thought* I knew was a fabrication – something to make me fall in love with,' I said bitterly.

'Unsuccessfully,' Bastion interjected.

'Very unsuccessfully,' I agreed. 'No man has turned my head in years until you.' I kissed him lightly. 'So, we need to go to Caernarfon Castle.'

He blinked at the change of subject. 'Why?'

'I need to see a man about a dog.'

Chapter 55

In the end we flew Griffin Air despite Oscar and Benji's protests. We left them to debrief Ethan and disseminate news of Jeb's betrayal. It was nice to be alone with Bastion again, to have nothing around us but air and sun. It felt entirely too long since we'd had time to ourselves but this would have to do. When all this was over, I was renting us a cabin on a beach and we were going to drink cocktails and re-enact as many of the drinks as possible. An Orgasm followed by a Wallbanger sounded fun. A girl can dream.

The air was cool and I was feeling relaxed when we finally landed. We were met by a host of solemn brethren guards, all dressed in black, who escorted us into a small side office. Indy was in her Great Dane form; she was curled into a surprisingly small ball, blue-grey fur giving her an other-worldly feel even in her incognito mode.

She stretched as soon as we walked in and bounded to greet us. Her tail caught a mug on the desk and sent it flying. It broke on the hard wooden floor. The man behind the desk sighed. 'Another one bites the dust.'

Tom Smith is a fellow ginger but, unlike me, he is all hard muscle. His bulk has extra bulk – he is a tank of a man. Despite having very limited magic, I had no doubt he'd be one of the deadliest men in a room at any given time. Except when Bastion was there, of course.

I wondered if Tom was one of those griffins who were hidden as brethren then dismissed the thought. Emory had told me once that Tom Smith's family line had been a gift to him from his adoptive parents, Audrey and Cuthbert. And dragons can't lie.

Tom stood and offered his hand to Bastion, a rare gesture. Bastion took it and pulled him in for one of those manly hugs. They clapped each other on the shoulders and then drew back. 'Bastion,' Tom greeted him, laying a bit too much emphasis on his name.

A ghost of a smile touched Bastion's lips. I looked between them. 'What am I missing?'

'Tom used to know me by another name. He's still sulking about it.'

Tom glared. 'I do not *sulk*.'

'Could have fooled me,' Bastion said mildly, but then he spoiled it by shooting Tom a grin. 'How's things?'

Tom pinched his nose. 'Emory is never allowed to go on holiday ever again.'

'Are the dragon Council members not pulling their weight?' I asked as I stroked Indy's slightly bitey head. I fixed her with my best glare and she subsided, coming close so I could stroke her on a less toothy part of her body.

'The Council members are too busy playing games amongst themselves. Their political manoeuvring makes chess look easy,' Tom complained. 'And quite a few of the dark seraph are missing.'

There was genuine anxiety in his voice, which is why I decided to take pity on him. 'Reynard and a select few went to guard Emory and Jinx.'

Tom's jaw worked. 'So I've been wasting valuable resources trying to find four dark seraph that are actually dicking about in Thailand?'

'I don't know what they're doing there but yes, dicking about might be included.'

'Reynard and I are going to have words,' he promised darkly.

'Just don't do it near Shirdal,' I advised. 'He's all protective. It's sweet.'

Tom grimaced. 'Noted. I don't want to piss off Shirdal. Now, do you want the dog?' He gestured to Indy, who was still busy wagging at us with her whole bum.

At the mention of her name, she went to give me a lick across the face, 'No!' I said firmly. 'No kisses!'

She made a sad noise but went back to nuzzling me instead. This time she kept her teeth in check. 'Good girl,' I praised her. I knew first-hand how smart hellhounds are. I had spoken to Gato a number of times, albeit he is a special case.

'Indy,' I started, 'I'm here to see you. I need to make a potion to help my mum. She was in the third realm too much and her mind is fractured, lost in time. I need to brew her a potion, a potion that's never been made before. I think if I used something from you it might help her. I really need to speak to her and get some information from her. I wouldn't ask if it weren't essential. Can I take something from you – some hair, a nail clipping, perhaps? I won't use it for anything other than Mum's potion, you have my word and oath.'

Indy studied me for a long moment, her body tense and her tail eerily still. Then she strode to Bastion and nudged him firmly. He raised an eyebrow. 'What?' He didn't speak hellhound. Nor did I.

'She wants you to do something?' I guessed.

'Yes, but what?'

I shrugged. 'You're the one she's trying to talk to. You figure it out.'

Indy barked then batted his hand with her head. He looked at her for a moment before shifting his hand to his talons. She barked again, gave a wag then sat down and offered him a paw. Relief surged through me; she was offering her paw for clippings. She was willing to help.

'Thank you, Indy. Thank you so much.' I struggled to keep my emotions hidden. I couldn't have Tom reporting that I'd grown soft since my appointment as the Crone.

My words distracted her. She stood back up, came over to give me an enthusiastic lick on the face. This time I let her. I stroked her on her back and kissed her giant forehead. 'Thank you,' I repeated softly.

She wagged heartily before seeming to remember that she was supposed to be doing something else. She sat back down and held out her right forepaw again. Bastion carefully trimmed her nails and took a little patch of her fur. When he set her paw back down, she lifted it up again and pawed him firmly. He took a little more of her fur and looked at her quizzically. She barked at him.

'Look,' Bastion said, 'I'm just going to hold still. You do whatever you think you need to do with my talons, okay?'

Indy lifted her paw up and promptly used his claw to cut her front leg. Blood welled up. I hastily threw open my tote bag and rifled through it for an empty vial. I caught the blood as it dripped down her outstretched leg. 'Warn us next time!' I chastened.

She gave me a flat look.

'Sorry, you're right. Thanks. Just thanks.'

She gave me a satisfied look and a toothy grin. She hadn't cut herself too deeply and the blood soon slowed. She sat back down in her bed behind Tom's desk and carefully licked her paw. 'Do you want me to heal it?' I offered.

She snorted derisively and went back to licking, so I guessed that was a no. I stoppered the vial and stowed it carefully in my tote bag.

'You want me to arrange a helicopter ride home for you?' Tom offered politely.

'No, thank you. I like riding on Bastion.'

Tom snickered. 'I bet you do,' he muttered, smirking at Bastion.

Bastion's eyes narrowed and I heard the rumble of a growl. The smirk fled Tom's features. 'Touchy!' he noted, holding up his hands.

Bastion held his eyes a moment longer before stepping back. I heard Tom's little sigh of relief. They might be friendly, but Bastion wouldn't let *anyone* disrespect me. It gave me a warm, fuzzy feeling.

There was a chewing noise and we all turned to Indy. 'Indy!' Tom barked. 'Bad dog! Those are my inclement-weather boots!'

A grin tugged at my lips. 'You call your welly boots "inclement-weather boots"?' I did air quotes with my fingers.

The tops of his ears pinked and he cleared his throat. 'Welly boots seems a bit childish.'

'Gumboots?' Bastion suggested.

Another loud chew sounded and Tom gave an aggrieved sigh. 'She hates me.'

Indy barked and tapped her tail. 'She likes you,' I disagreed. 'She just really loves inclement-weather boots. Buy her some new chew toys.'

'Roger that.'

We said our goodbyes and flew home the same way we'd arrived. I had all of the flight to go over the flat look Bastion had given Tom on my behalf, so when we got home I made sure to show Bastion exactly how much I loved his protective urges.

Chapter 56

I got up early and consulted the DeLea potion bible. It didn't have a potion for anything like I needed, but I cobbled together a base by using a combination of three memory and mind healing bases together. There was a lot of overlap; but apart from removing a couple of ingredients that could have had explosive consequences, I put them together without too much difficulty.

When I added Indy's gifts depended on how the potion progressed. There were a couple of variations I could go with, so I decided to split the prepared base into four. I'd add the hair to one, the claw clippings to another and the blood to the third. The fourth would get a bit of everything.

I had already tasked Oscar with meeting with Mum and getting a small sample of her blood so we could key the potion directly to her. He was due back any minute and I was antsy to get to the next stage of brewing.

I took a deep breath and calmed my mind. Hurrying could ruin everything; perfection takes time. I blew out my breath and turned up the fire a little. When the colour was uniform, it was ready to be split.

I carefully decanted the hot liquid into four small pewter cauldrons and let them cool slightly. Satisfied they were stable, I went to my office to see if Oscar was back. He was talking quietly to Bastion, who had Fehu sitting on his shoulder.

'Hey, Fehu!' I called. I wondered where he'd been – I'd missed his feathery presence. He gave a kraa and leapt from Bastion's shoulder onto mine. I gave his jet-black feathers a stroke. 'It's good to see you,' I murmured.

I felt a rush of warmth and affection that wasn't my own. My eyes widened as I realised it wasn't Bastion's feelings I was experiencing but Fehu's. Somehow lifting the suppression rune from our bond had also let me feel Fehu, too.

'I can feel him,' I blurted to Bastion. 'Fehu! I can feel him!' I was grinning from ear to ear.

Fehu nuzzled me, tangling in my red hair and peeking through the loose strands. That was what I'd always imagined a bond with a familiar would be like. I didn't regret being bonded with Bastion, not for a second, but it wasn't like I could keep him in my pocket like Ria kept her familiar Fido, or twirled around my wrist like Hannah kept Fifi.

I felt a wave of pleasure from Bastion. 'You don't mind?' I asked. Some might feel aggrieved to share a familiar, especially one like Fehu who had been bonded with Bastion for more than a century.

'Not at all,' he said lightly. 'I hoped something like this might happen. The way Fehu always acted around you, I wondered if there was something there but these things can take time.'

Oscar smiled. 'I'm glad for you, Amber.'

'Thank you.' I stroked Fehu's little head again. 'Did everything go okay with Mum? Did she give you the blood?'

The smile slid off his face. 'She didn't know me, so I asked Charlize to take it. Your mum gave it willingly to her.' He handed me a small bag of blood.

'Thanks.' I stepped forward and hugged him. 'I'm sorry she didn't know you.' Oscar hadn't wanted to take her blood; he seemed resigned to my potion failing, which seemed oddly defeatist. I hoped I'd prove him wrong.

'Can you get me an appointment with Liyana?' I asked Bastion. No doubt the Seer High Priestess would be busy, but at least I could tell her that I'd found and killed Melva's murderer – and get my potion tested.

'Consider it done,' Bastion said lightly.

'Thank you.' I brushed my lips against his forehead before heading back into my office and the laboratory behind it. I'd just stepped into it when Benji slid out of the walls. I gasped and held a hand to my heart. 'By the Goddess, Benji, you scared the life out of me! I didn't realise you could move through the walls here, too. I thought it was an Edinburgh thing.'

'It's harder,' he admitted, 'but not impossible.'

'What's up?'

'I'm feeling lonely,' he said abruptly.

'I'm sorry to hear that,' I said softly. 'Lonely is not fun. Are you missing David?'

'I believe I am. I liked teaching him things. It made me feel important.'

'You are important,' I insisted. 'In lots of ways.' I set down the small bag of blood carefully. 'Would you like a hug?'

'Yes please, Am Bam. Perhaps it will stop this ache.'

That gave a hard tug at my heartstrings. I pulled him close and he returned the gesture, tucking my head under his chin. His cold touch leached into my skin but I held on; he wasn't ready to let go and I wasn't ready to let him down. I'd been lonely more times than I could count.

I wracked my brains for what people were supposed to do when someone felt low. 'Cup of tea?' I offered.

A smile traced his lips. 'That would be nice but finish your potion first. I'll watch quietly. Your company will be enough to make me happy.'

Benji pulled out a bar stool and sat down, then watched me bustle around, fiddling with ingredients and the height of the flame. I checked the temperature: it was perfect for ingredient combination, so I added Mum's blood to each cauldron. Then I added each variation of ingredient to the three waiting cauldrons, and all three to the fourth cauldron.

I stirred patiently. When the potions turned silver, I knew they were done. I had already prepared the ice bath, so I transferred the cauldrons to it and heard the hiss as the heat hit the cold. I started to stir each of them in turn.

'Can I help?' Benji offered solicitously.

I am not good at delegating but I surprised myself by nodding. 'Sure. You can stir these two.'

He joined me by the ice bath and together we stirred the cauldrons. It was easier with the two of us working together. My necklace was warm on my neck. I touched it lightly and felt a roll of approval from my sisters.

It had taken me a long time, but maybe I was finally learning how to play nicely with others.

Never fear! *Destiny of the Witch* is coming soon! Don't forget to pre-order the final instalment of this witchy saga.

To tide you over, here is a free bonus scene from Bastion's point of view:

https://dl.bookfunnel.com/m9xqy2tf4v

This scene has spoilers for *Familiar of the Witch,* so don't read the bonus scene until you've read *Familiar of the Witch. Enjoy!*

Other Works by Heather

The *Portlock Paranormal Detective* Series with Jilleen Dolbeare

The Vampire and the Case of her Dastardly Death - Book 0.5 (a prequel story),

The Vampire and the Case of the Wayward Werewolf – Book 1,

The Vampire and the Case of the Secretive Siren – Book 2,

The Vampire and the Case of the Baleful Banshee – Book 3.

The Vampire and the Case of the Cursed Canine – Book 4

The *Other Realm* series

Glimmer of Dragons- Book 0.5 (a prequel story),

Glimmer of The Other- Book 1,

Glimmer of Hope- Book 2,

Glimmer of Christmas – Book 2.5 (a Christmas tale),

Glimmer of Death – Book 3,

Glimmer of Deception – Book 4,

It is recommended that you read *The Other Wolf series* before continuing with:

Challenge of the Court– Book 5,

Betrayal of the Court– Book 6; and

Revival of the Court– Book 7.

The *Other Wolf* Series

Defender of The Pack– Book 0.5 (a prequel story),

Protection of the Pack– Book 1,

Guardians of the Pack– Book 2; and

Saviour of The Pack– Book 3.

The *Other Witch* Series

Rune of the Witch – Book 0.5 (a prequel story),

Hex of the Witch– Book 1,

Coven of the Witch;– Book 2,

Familiar of the Witch– Book 3, and

Destiny of the Witch – Book 4.

About Heather

Heather is an urban fantasy writer and mum. She was born and raised near Windsor, which gave her the misguided impression that she was close to royalty in some way. She is not, though she once got a letter from Queen Elizabeth II's lady-in-waiting.

Heather went to university in Liverpool, where she took up skydiving and met her future husband. When she's not running around after her children, she's plotting her next book and daydreaming about vampires, dragons and kick-ass heroines.

Heather is a book lover who grew up reading Brian Jacques and Anne McCaffrey. She loves to travel and once spent a month in Thailand. She vows to return.

Want to learn more about Heather? Subscribe to her newsletter for behind-the-scenes scoops, free bonus material and a cheeky peek into her world. Her subscribers will always get the heads up about the best deals on her books.

Subscribe to her Newsletter at her website www.heatherg harris.com/subscribe.

Heather's Patreon

Heather has started her very own Patreon page. What is Patreon? It's a subscription service that allows you to support Heather AND read her books way before anyone else! For a small monthly fee you could be reading Heather's next book, on a weekly chapter-by-chapter basis (in its roughest draft form!) in the next week or two. If you hit "Join the community" you can follow Heather along for FREE, though you won't get access to all the good stuff, like early release books, polls, live Q&A's, character art and more! You can even have a video call with Heather or have a character named after you! Heather's current patrons are getting to read a novella called House Bound which isn't available anywhere else, not even to her newsletter subscribers!

If you're too impatient to wait until Heather's next release, then Patreon is made for you.

Contact Heather

Website: www.heathergharris.com

Email: HeatherGHarrisAuthor@gmail.com

Reviews

Reviews feed Heather's soul. She'd really appreciate it if you could take a few moments to review her books on Amazon, Bookbub, or Goodreads and say hello.

About Heather

Heather is an urban fantasy writer and mum. She was born and raised near Windsor, which gave her the misguided impression that she was close to royalty in some way. She is not, though she once got a letter from Queen Elizabeth II's lady-in-waiting.

Heather went to university in Liverpool, where she took up skydiving and met her future husband. When she's not running around after her children, she's plotting her next book and daydreaming about vampires, dragons and kick-ass heroines.

Heather is a book lover who grew up reading Brian Jacques and Anne McCaffrey. She loves to travel and once spent a month in Thailand. She vows to return.

Want to learn more about Heather? Subscribe to her newsletter for behind-the-scenes scoops, free bonus material and a cheeky peek into her world. Her subscribers will always get the heads up about the best deals on her books.

Subscribe to her Newsletter at her website www.heathergharris.com/subscribe.

Too impatient to wait for Heather's next book? Join her (ever growing!) army of supportive patrons at Patreon.

Heather's Patreon

Heather has started her very own Patreon page. What is Patreon? It's a subscription service that allows you to support Heather AND read her books way before anyone else! For a small monthly fee you could be reading Heather's next book, on a weekly chapter-by-chapter basis (in its roughest draft form!) in the next week or two. If you hit "Join the community" you can follow Heather along for FREE, though you won't get access to all the good stuff, like early release books, polls, live Q&A's, character art and more! You can even have a video call with Heather or have a character named after you! Heather's current patrons are getting to read a novella called House Bound which isn't available anywhere else, not even to her newsletter subscribers!

If you're too impatient to wait until Heather's next release, then Patreon is made for you! Join Heather's patrons here.

Heather's Shop and YouTube Channel

Heather now has her very own online shop! There you can buy oodles of glorious merchandise and audiobooks directly from her. Heather's audiobooks will still be on sale elsewhere, of course, but Heather pays her audiobook narrator *and* her cover designer - she makes the entire product - and then Audible pays her 25%. OUCH. Where possible, Heather would love it if you would buy her audiobooks directly from her, and then she can keep an amazing 90% of the money instead. Which she can reinvest in more books, in every form! But Audiobooks aren't all there is in the shop. You can get hoodies, t-shirts, mugs and more! Go and check her store out at: https://shop.heathergharris.com/

And if you don't have spare money to pay for audiobooks, Heather would still love you to experience Alyse Gibb's expert rendition of the books. You can listen to Heather's audiobooks for free on her YouTube Channel: https://www.youtube.com/@HeatherGHarrisAuthor

Stay in Touch

Heather has been working hard on a bunch of cool things, including a new and shiny website which you'll love. Check it out at www.heathergharris.com.

If you want to hear about all Heather's latest releases – subscribe to her newsletter for news, fun and freebies. Subscribe at Heather's website www.heathergharris.com/subscribe.

Contact Info: www.heathergharris.com

Email: HeatherGHarrisAuthor@gmail.com

Social Media

Heather can also be found on a host of social medias:

Facebook Page

Facebook Reader Group

Goodreads

Bookbub

Instagram

If you get a chance, please do follow Heather on Amazon!

Reviews

Reviews feed Heather's soul. She'd really appreciate it if you could take a few moments to review her books on Amazon,

Bookbub, or Goodreads and say hello.

www.ingramcontent.com/pod-product-compliance
Lightning Source LLC
Chambersburg PA
CBHW061623210726
48287CB00001B/259